Melusine

The Vampires' Ball

Written by: GILSON
Illustrated by: CLARKE
Colour work: Cerise

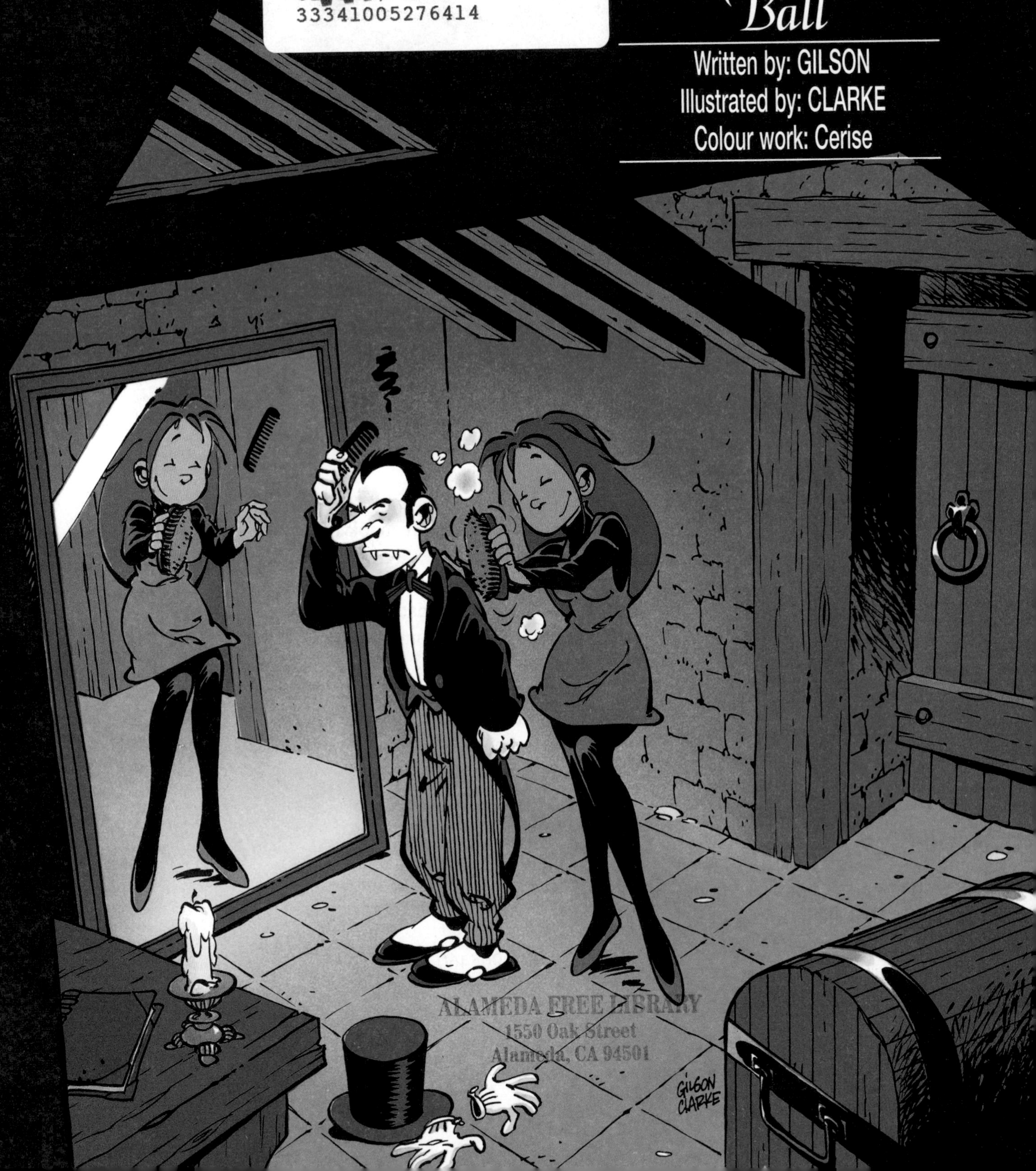
GILSON
CLARKE

Original title: Mélusine 2 – Le Bal des vampires

Original edition: © Dupuis, 1995
by Clarke & Gilson
www.dupuis.com

English translation: © 2008 Cinebook Ltd

Translator: Jerome Saincantin
Lettering and text layout: Imadjinn sarl
Printed in Spain by Just Colour Graphic

This edition first published in Great Britain in 2008 by
CINEBOOK Ltd
56 Beech Avenue
Canterbury, Kent
CT4 7TA
www.cinebook.com

A CIP catalogue record for this book
is available from the British Library

ISBN 978-1-905460-69-4

9th CINEBOOK
The 9th Art Publisher

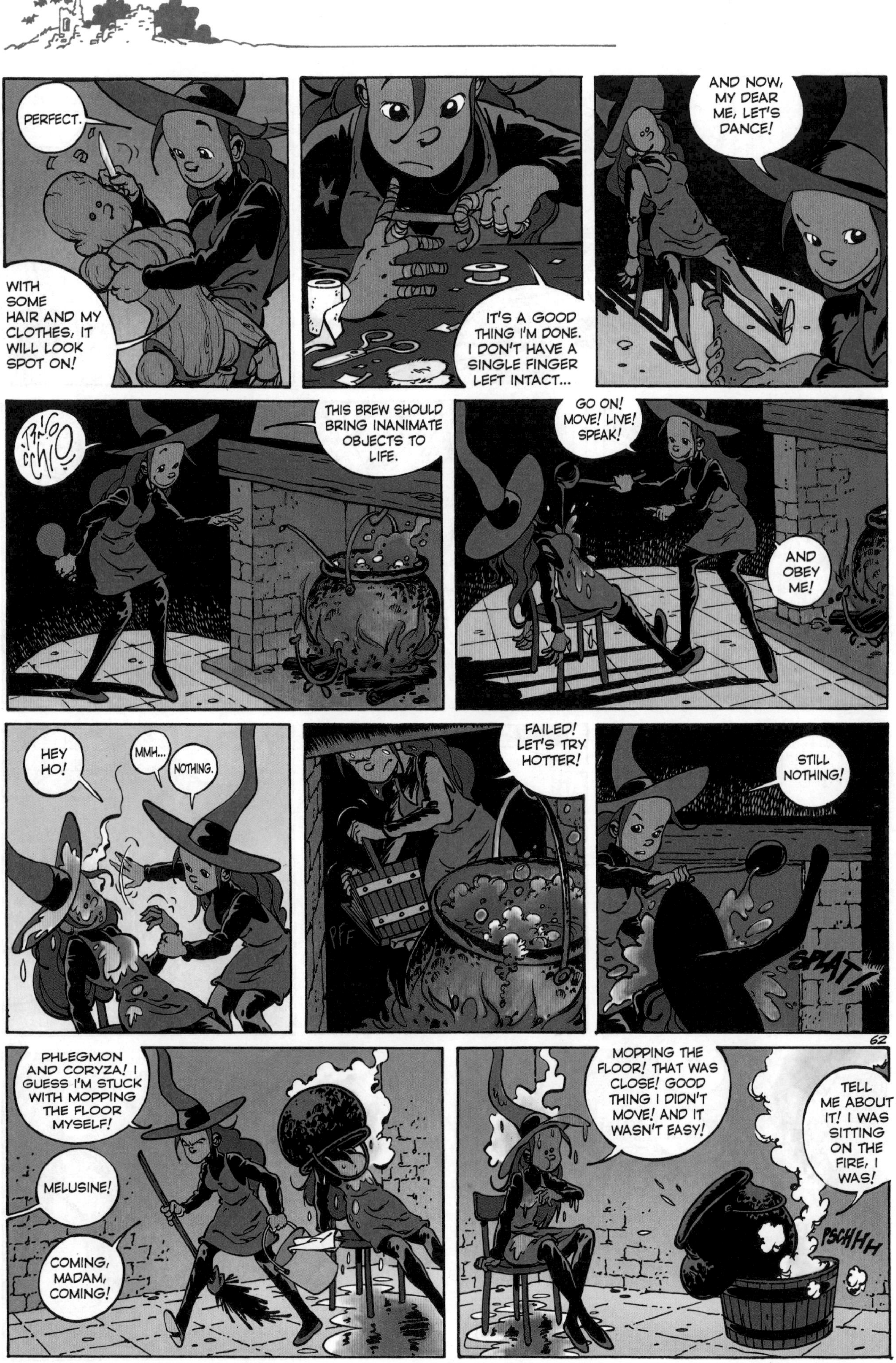
PERFECT.
WITH SOME HAIR AND MY CLOTHES, IT WILL LOOK SPOT ON!
IT'S A GOOD THING I'M DONE. I DON'T HAVE A SINGLE FINGER LEFT INTACT...
AND NOW, MY DEAR ME, LET'S DANCE!
THIS BREW SHOULD BRING INANIMATE OBJECTS TO LIFE.
GO ON! MOVE! LIVE! SPEAK!
AND OBEY ME!
HEY HO!
MMH...
NOTHING.
FAILED! LET'S TRY HOTTER!
PFF
STILL NOTHING!
SPLAT!
PHLEGMON AND CORYZA! I GUESS I'M STUCK WITH MOPPING THE FLOOR MYSELF!
MELUSINE!
COMING, MADAM, COMING!
MOPPING THE FLOOR! THAT WAS CLOSE! GOOD THING I DIDN'T MOVE! AND IT WASN'T EASY!
TELL ME ABOUT IT! I WAS SITTING ON THE FIRE, I WAS!
PSCHHH

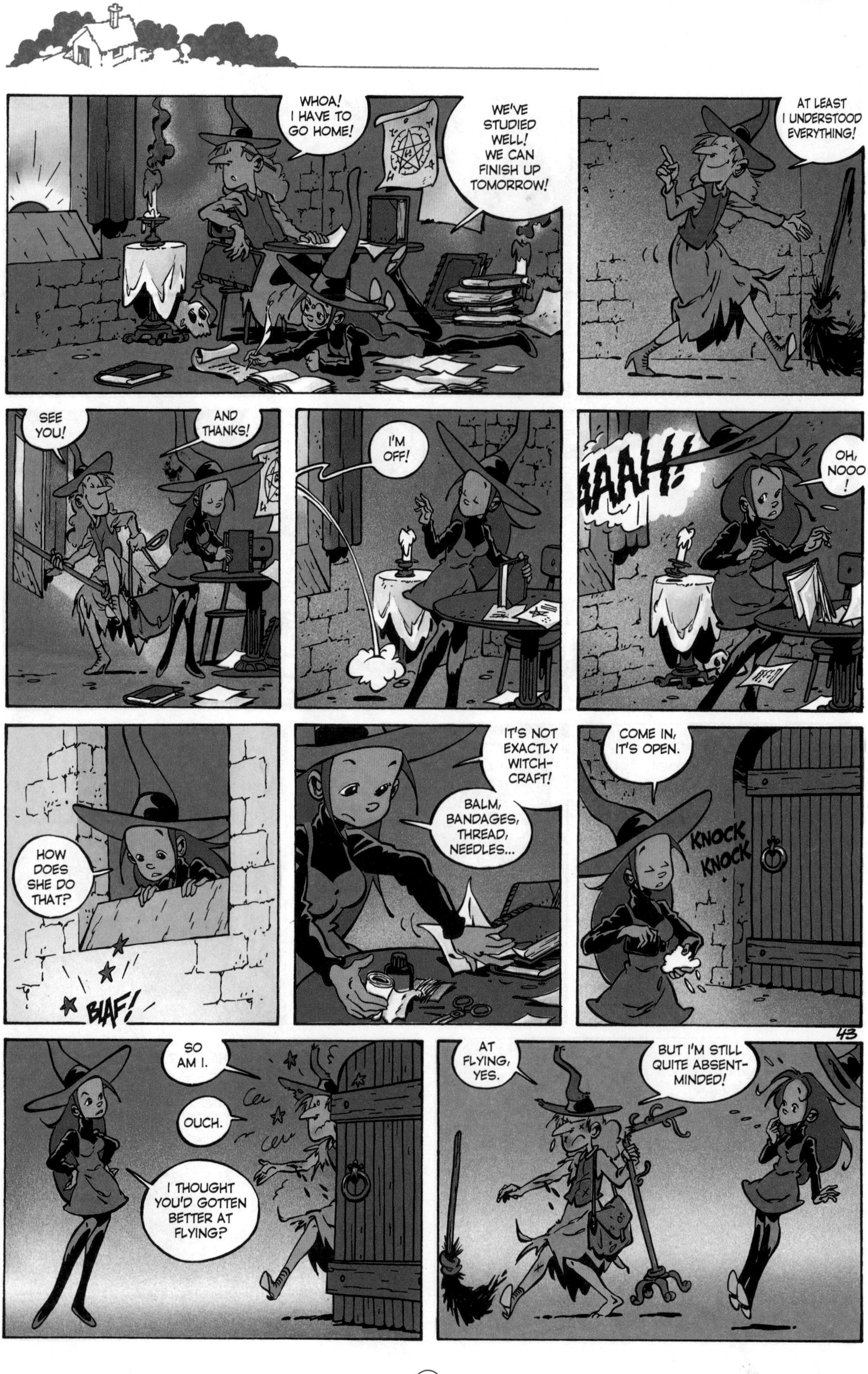
WHOA! I HAVE TO GO HOME!
WE'VE STUDIED WELL! WE CAN FINISH UP TOMORROW!
AT LEAST I UNDERSTOOD EVERYTHING!
SEE YOU!
AND THANKS!
I'M OFF!
AAAH!
OH, NOOO!
HOW DOES SHE DO THAT?
BLAF!
IT'S NOT EXACTLY WITCH-CRAFT!
BALM, BANDAGES, THREAD, NEEDLES...
COME IN, IT'S OPEN.
KNOCK KNOCK
43
SO AM I.
OUCH.
I THOUGHT YOU'D GOTTEN BETTER AT FLYING?
AT FLYING, YES.
BUT I'M STILL QUITE ABSENT-MINDED!

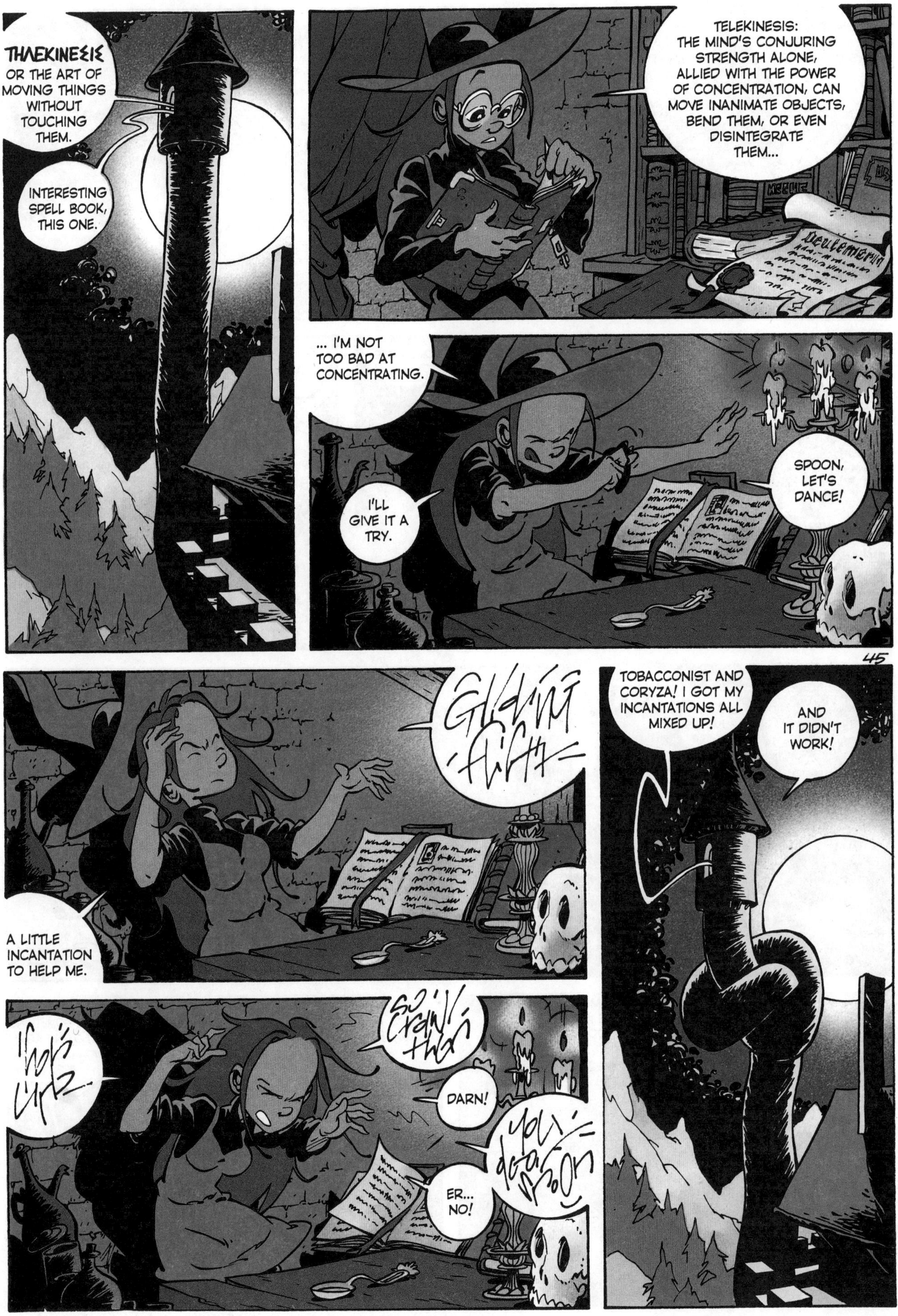
ΤΗΛΕΚΙΝΕΣΙΣ
OR THE ART OF MOVING THINGS WITHOUT TOUCHING THEM.
INTERESTING SPELL BOOK, THIS ONE.
TELEKINESIS: THE MIND'S CONJURING STRENGTH ALONE, ALLIED WITH THE POWER OF CONCENTRATION, CAN MOVE INANIMATE OBJECTS, BEND THEM, OR EVEN DISINTEGRATE THEM...
... I'M NOT TOO BAD AT CONCENTRATING.
I'LL GIVE IT A TRY.
SPOON, LET'S DANCE!
A LITTLE INCANTATION TO HELP ME.
TOBACCONIST AND CORYZA! I GOT MY INCANTATIONS ALL MIXED UP!
AND IT DIDN'T WORK!
DARN!
ER... NO!

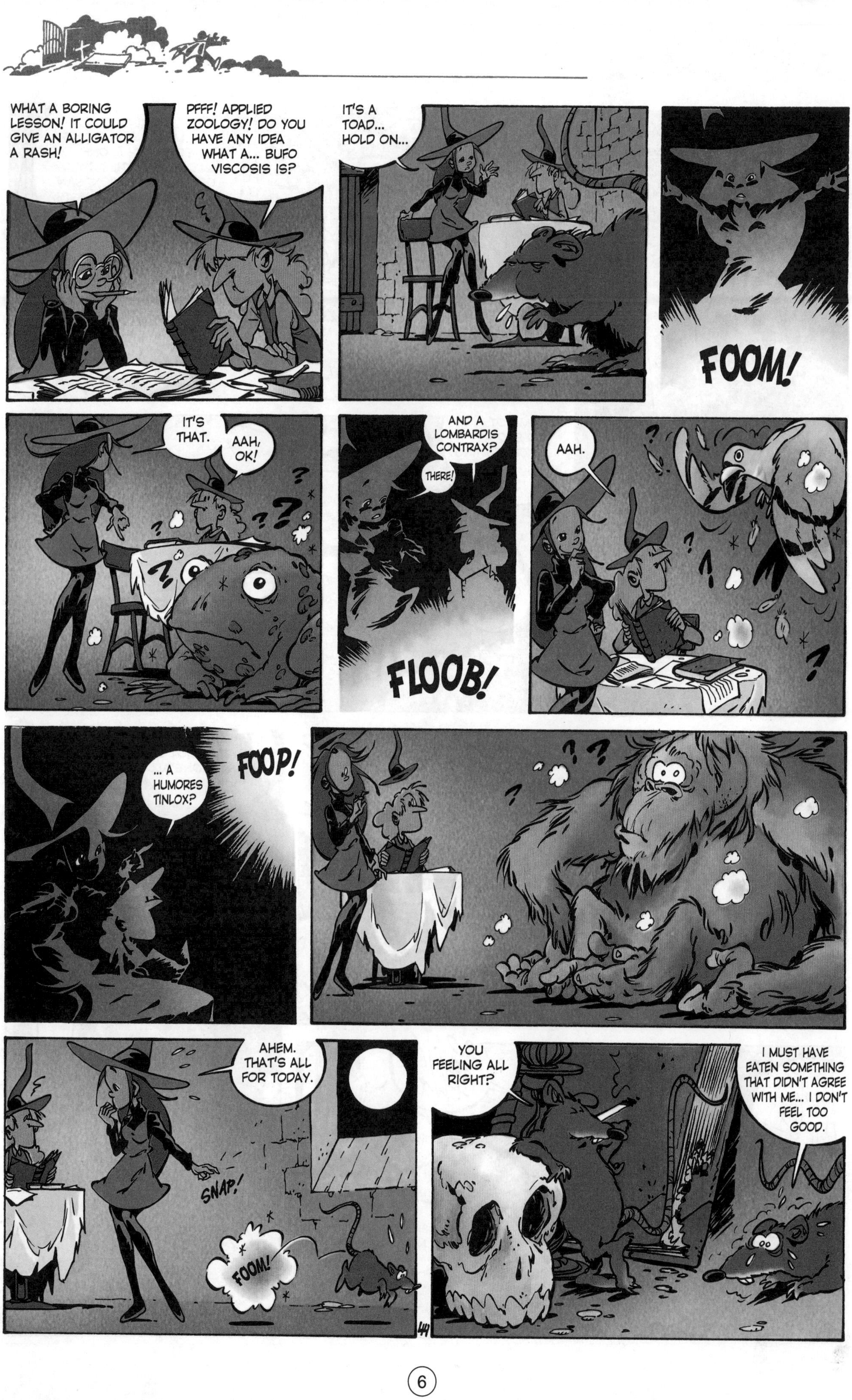
WHAT A BORING LESSON! IT COULD GIVE AN ALLIGATOR A RASH!
PFFF! APPLIED ZOOLOGY! DO YOU HAVE ANY IDEA WHAT A... BUFO VISCOSIS IS?
IT'S A TOAD... HOLD ON...
FOOM!
IT'S THAT.
AAH, OK!
AND A LOMBARDIS CONTRAX?
THERE!
FLOOB!
AAH.
... A HUMORES TINLOX?
FOOP!
AHEM. THAT'S ALL FOR TODAY.
SNAP!
FOOM!
YOU FEELING ALL RIGHT?
I MUST HAVE EATEN SOMETHING THAT DIDN'T AGREE WITH ME... I DON'T FEEL TOO GOOD.

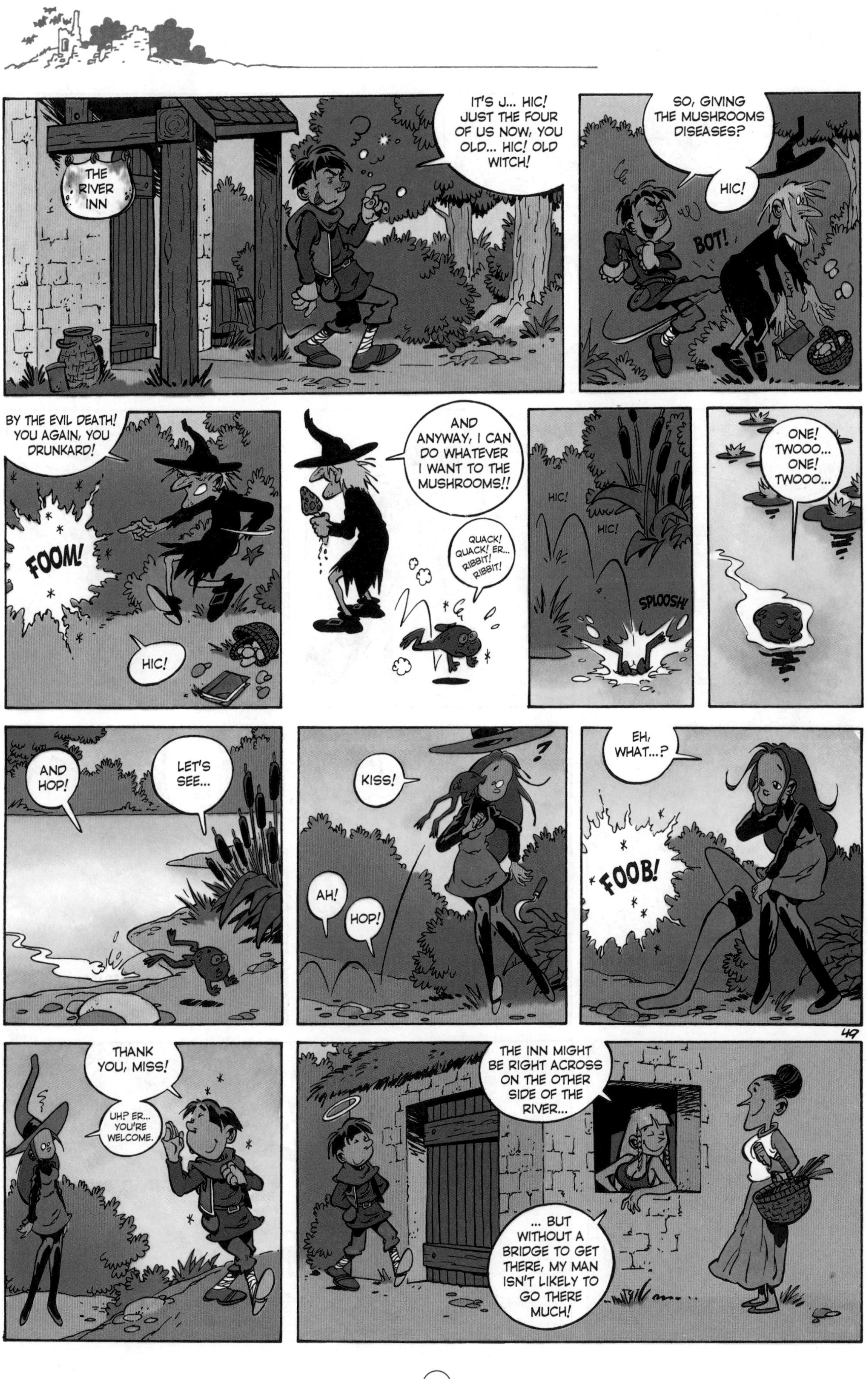
THE RIVER INN
IT'S J... HIC! JUST THE FOUR OF US NOW, YOU OLD... HIC! OLD WITCH!
SO, GIVING THE MUSHROOMS DISEASES?
HIC!
BOT!
BY THE EVIL DEATH! YOU AGAIN, YOU DRUNKARD!
FOOM!
HIC!
AND ANYWAY, I CAN DO WHATEVER I WANT TO THE MUSHROOMS!!
QUACK! QUACK! ER... RIBBIT! RIBBIT!
HIC!
HIC!
SPLOOSH!
ONE! TWOOO... ONE! TWOOO...
AND HOP!
LET'S SEE...
KISS!
AH!
HOP!
EH, WHAT...?
FOOB!
THANK YOU, MISS!
UH? ER... YOU'RE WELCOME.
THE INN MIGHT BE RIGHT ACROSS ON THE OTHER SIDE OF THE RIVER...
... BUT WITHOUT A BRIDGE TO GET THERE, MY MAN ISN'T LIKELY TO GO THERE MUCH!

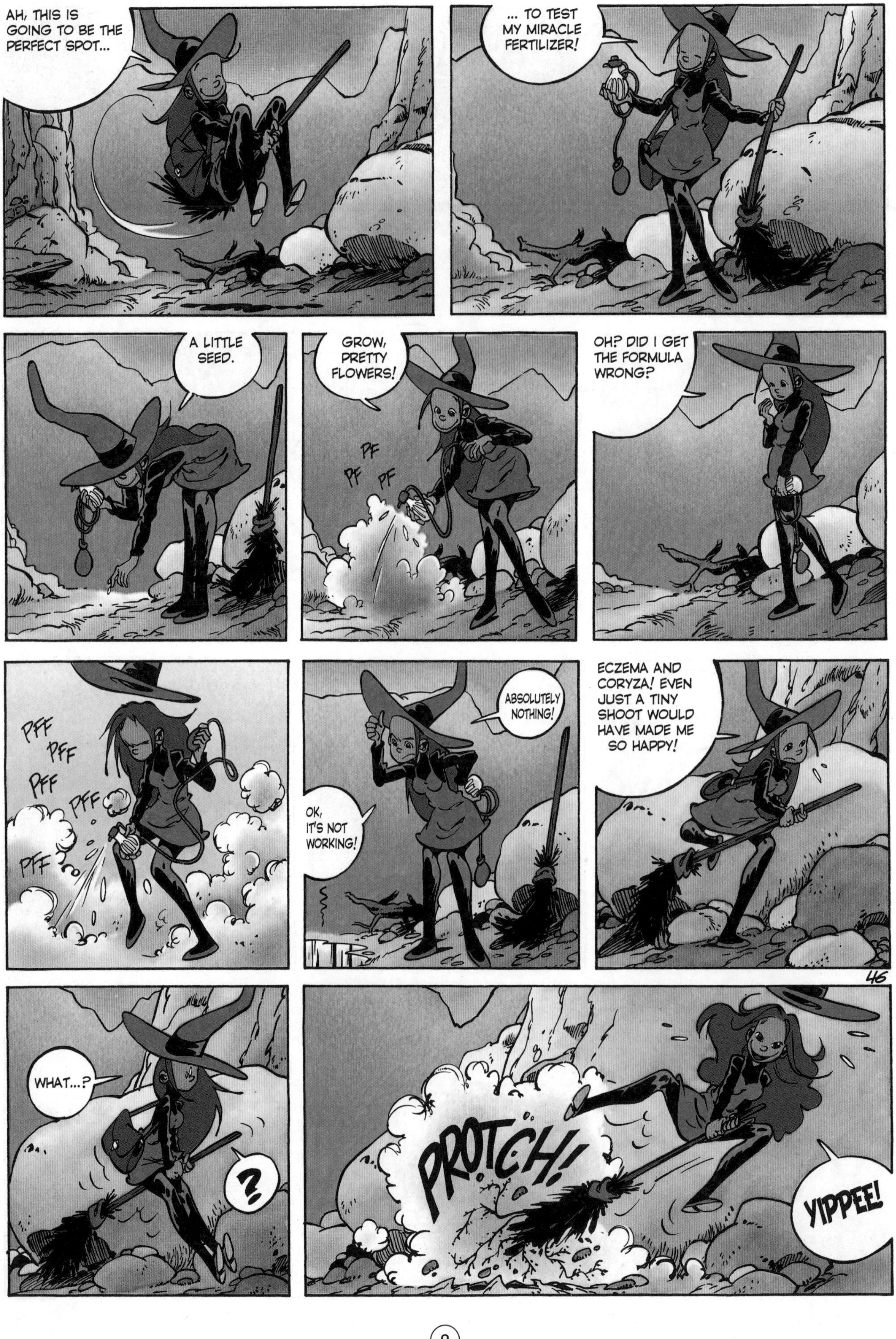
AH, THIS IS GOING TO BE THE PERFECT SPOT...
... TO TEST MY MIRACLE FERTILIZER!
A LITTLE SEED.
GROW, PRETTY FLOWERS!
PF PF PF
OH? DID I GET THE FORMULA WRONG?
PFF PFF PFF PFF PFF
ABSOLUTELY NOTHING!
OK, IT'S NOT WORKING!
ECZEMA AND CORYZA! EVEN JUST A TINY SHOOT WOULD HAVE MADE ME SO HAPPY!
46
WHAT...?
?
PROTCH!
YIPPEE!

OK, CANCRELUNE, PULL UP NOW.

PULL UP.

FOR GOODNESS' SAKE, PULL UP!

WHAM

OH, ENOUGH! IT'S OVER! YOU CAN LOOK NOW!

52

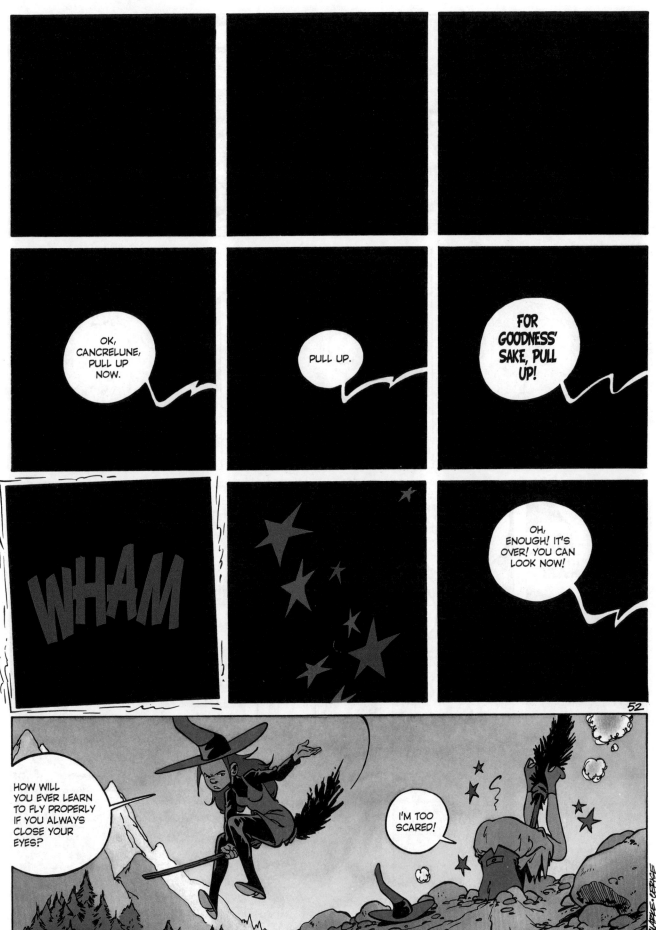

HOW WILL YOU EVER LEARN TO FLY PROPERLY IF YOU ALWAYS CLOSE YOUR EYES?

I'M TOO SCARED!

WITCH!

TO THE STAKE!

BAM! BAM!

I HATE SHOPPING IN THAT VILLAGE OF LOONIES!

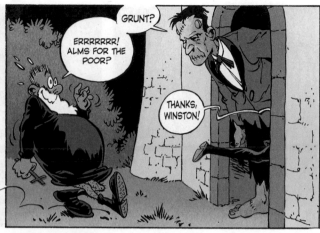

GRUNT?

ERRRRRRR! ALMS FOR THE POOR?

THANKS, WINSTON!

SO, MELUSINE, DID YOU PURCHASE THE SUPPLIES?

YES, MADAM.

ALL THAT? BUT THESE ARE LUXURY PRODUCTS, GIRL!

?

BUT MADAM, I NEEDED ALL THIS FOR THE CLEANING JOB YOU'VE GIVEN ME!

GIVE ME MY CHANGE, PLEASE.

55

THERE. IT CAME TO THREE SILVER LEI...

HOW MUCH?

IF I WEREN'T ALREADY DEAD, I'D CROAK HERE AND NOW! DO YOU WANT TO RUIN OUR FAMILY?

BUT I...

THAT'S ENOUGH! GO AND DO YOUR WORK.

Y... YES, MADAM

BEING THAT STINGY, THAT'S JUST UNBELIEVABLE!

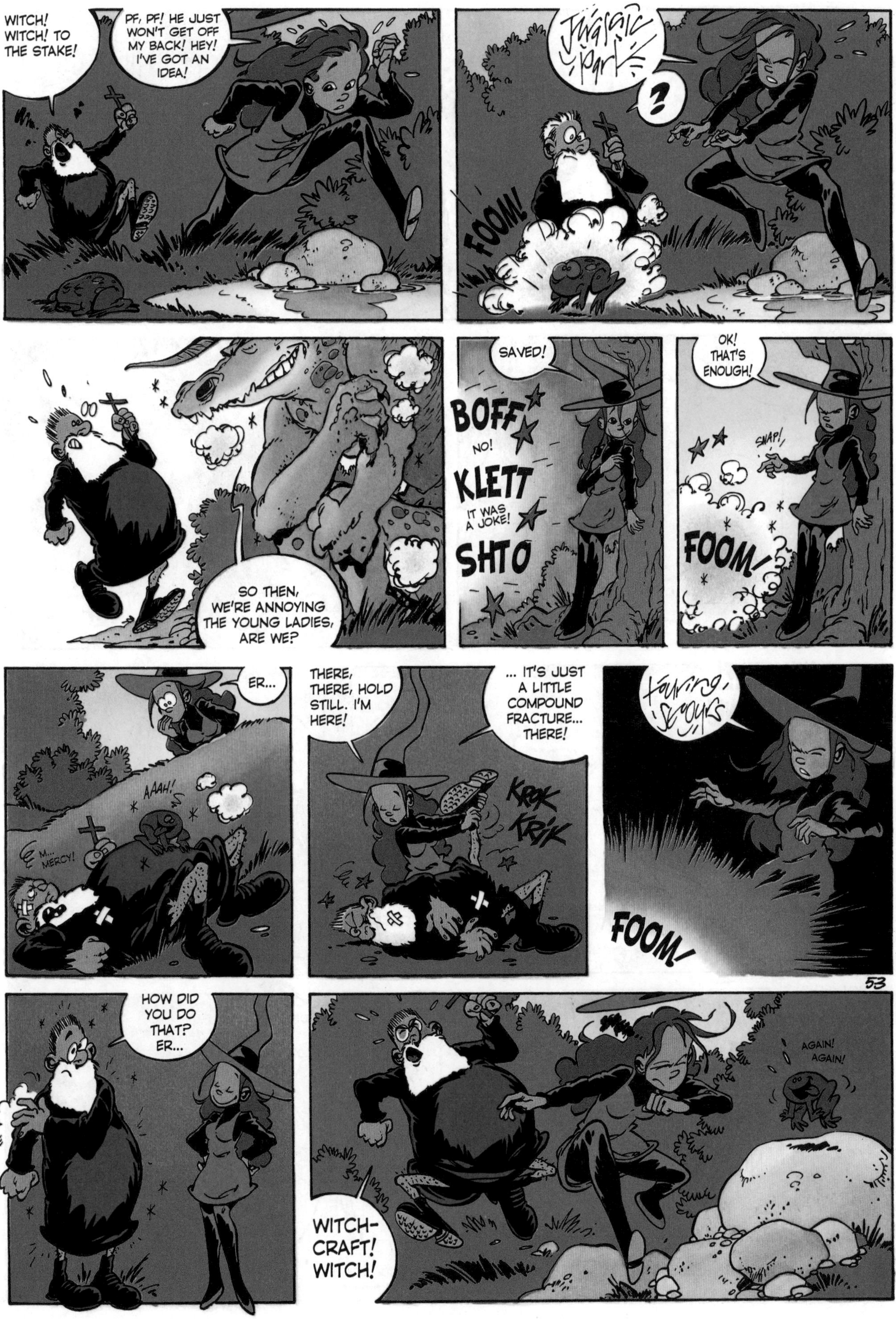
WITCH! WITCH! TO THE STAKE!
PF, PF! HE JUST WON'T GET OFF MY BACK! HEY! I'VE GOT AN IDEA!
Jurassic Park
?
FOOM!
SO THEN, WE'RE ANNOYING THE YOUNG LADIES, ARE WE?
SAVED!
BOFF
NO!
KLETT
IT WAS A JOKE!
SHTO
OK! THAT'S ENOUGH!
SNAP!
FOOM!
ER...
AAAH!
M... MERCY!
THERE, THERE, HOLD STILL. I'M HERE!
... IT'S JUST A LITTLE COMPOUND FRACTURE... THERE!
KROK
KRIK
FOOM!
53
HOW DID YOU DO THAT? ER...
AGAIN! AGAIN!
WITCH-CRAFT! WITCH!

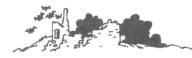

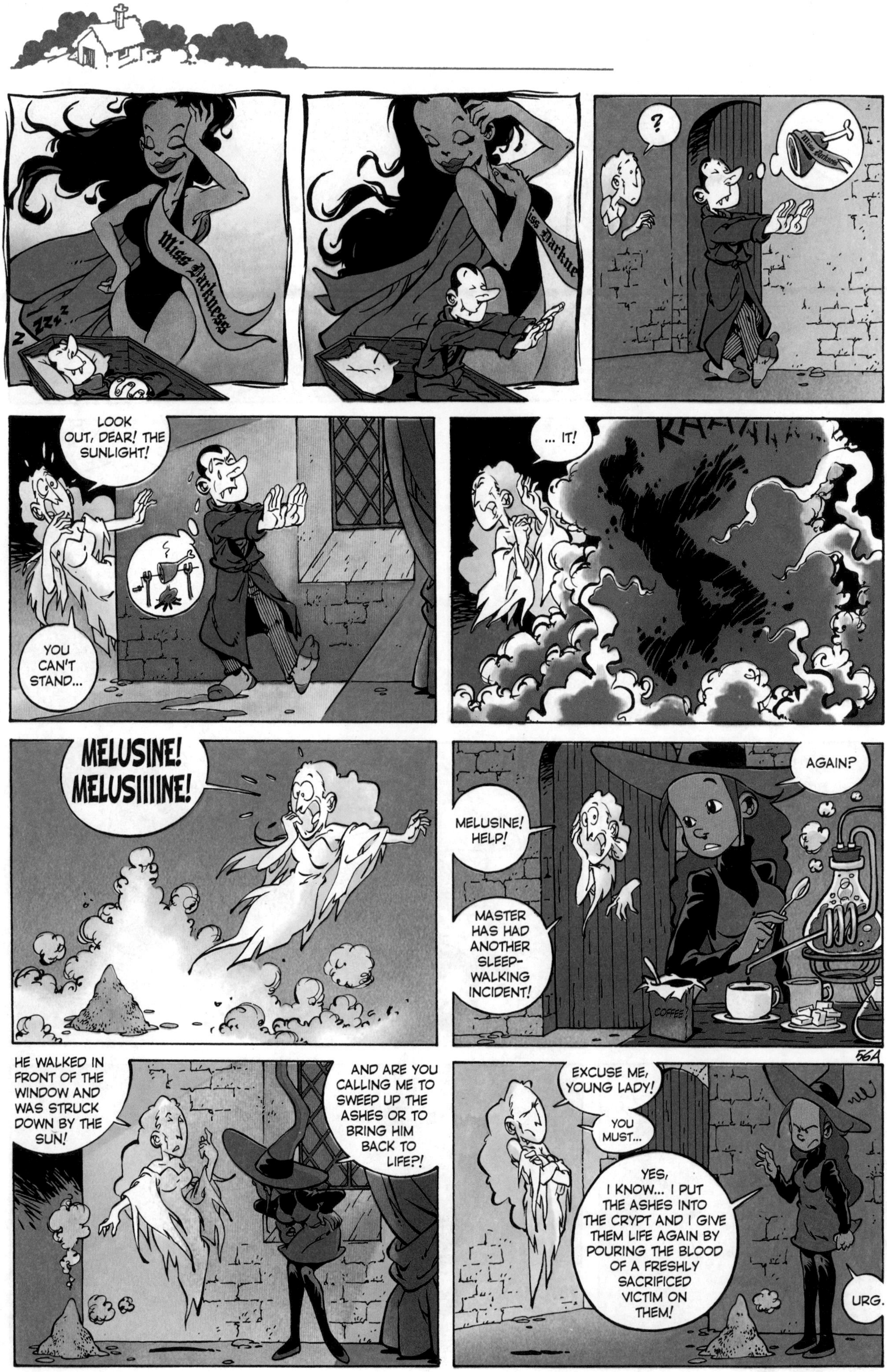
Miss Darkness
ZZZ
Miss Darkne
?
Miss Darkness
LOOK OUT, DEAR! THE SUNLIGHT!
YOU CAN'T STAND...
... IT!
MELUSINE! MELUSIIIINE!
AGAIN?
MELUSINE! HELP!
MASTER HAS HAD ANOTHER SLEEP-WALKING INCIDENT!
COFFEE
HE WALKED IN FRONT OF THE WINDOW AND WAS STRUCK DOWN BY THE SUN!
AND ARE YOU CALLING ME TO SWEEP UP THE ASHES OR TO BRING HIM BACK TO LIFE?!
EXCUSE ME, YOUNG LADY!
YOU MUST...
YES, I KNOW... I PUT THE ASHES INTO THE CRYPT AND I GIVE THEM LIFE AGAIN BY POURING THE BLOOD OF A FRESHLY SACRIFICED VICTIM ON THEM!
URG.

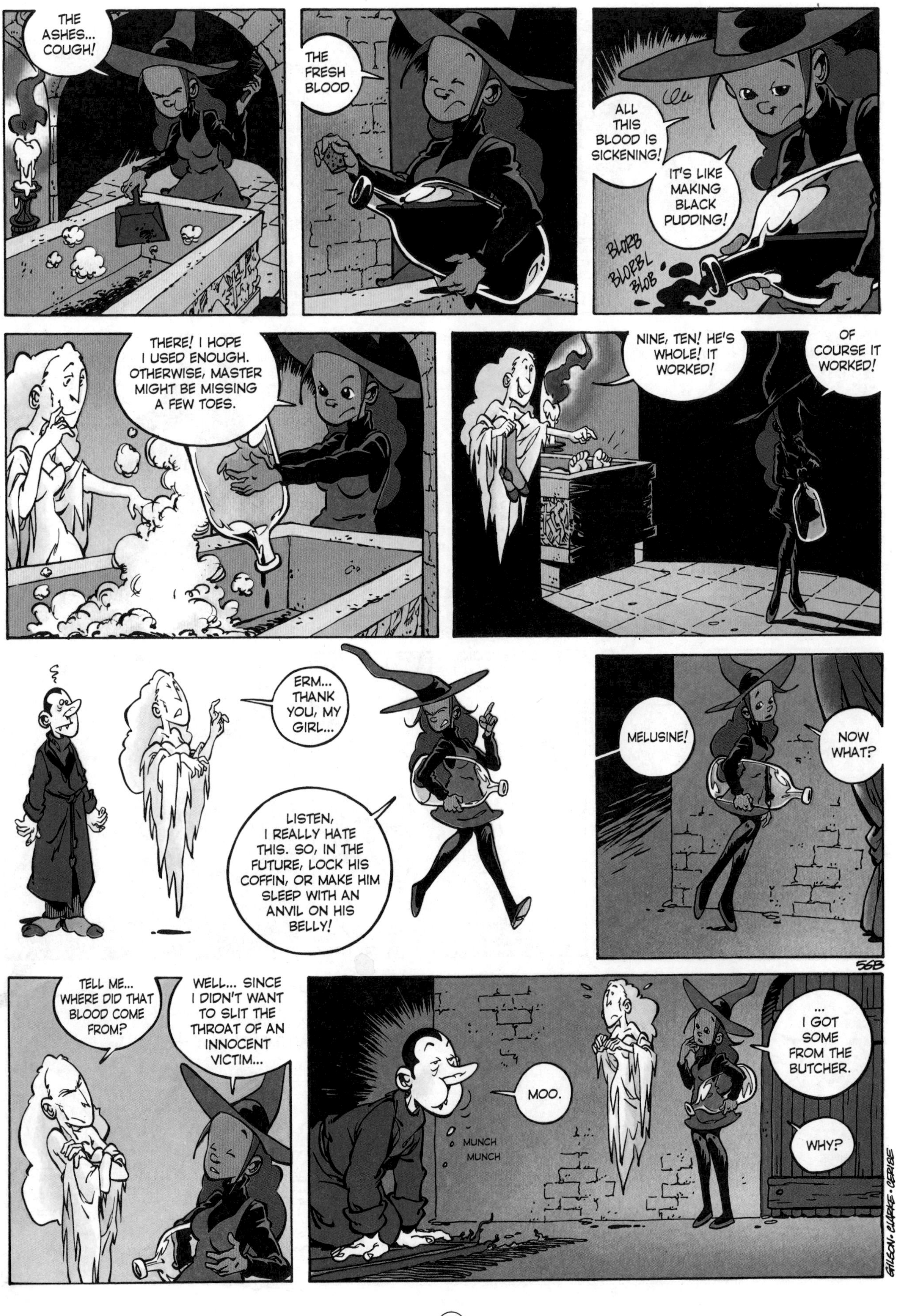
THE ASHES... COUGH!
THE FRESH BLOOD.
ALL THIS BLOOD IS SICKENING!
IT'S LIKE MAKING BLACK PUDDING!
BLORB BLORBL BLOB
THERE! I HOPE I USED ENOUGH. OTHERWISE, MASTER MIGHT BE MISSING A FEW TOES.
NINE, TEN! HE'S WHOLE! IT WORKED!
OF COURSE IT WORKED!
ERM... THANK YOU, MY GIRL...
LISTEN, I REALLY HATE THIS. SO, IN THE FUTURE, LOCK HIS COFFIN, OR MAKE HIM SLEEP WITH AN ANVIL ON HIS BELLY!
MELUSINE!
NOW WHAT?
TELL ME... WHERE DID THAT BLOOD COME FROM?
WELL... SINCE I DIDN'T WANT TO SLIT THE THROAT OF AN INNOCENT VICTIM...
MOO.
MUNCH MUNCH
... I GOT SOME FROM THE BUTCHER.
WHY?
GILSON • CLARKE • CERISE

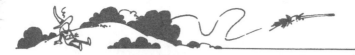

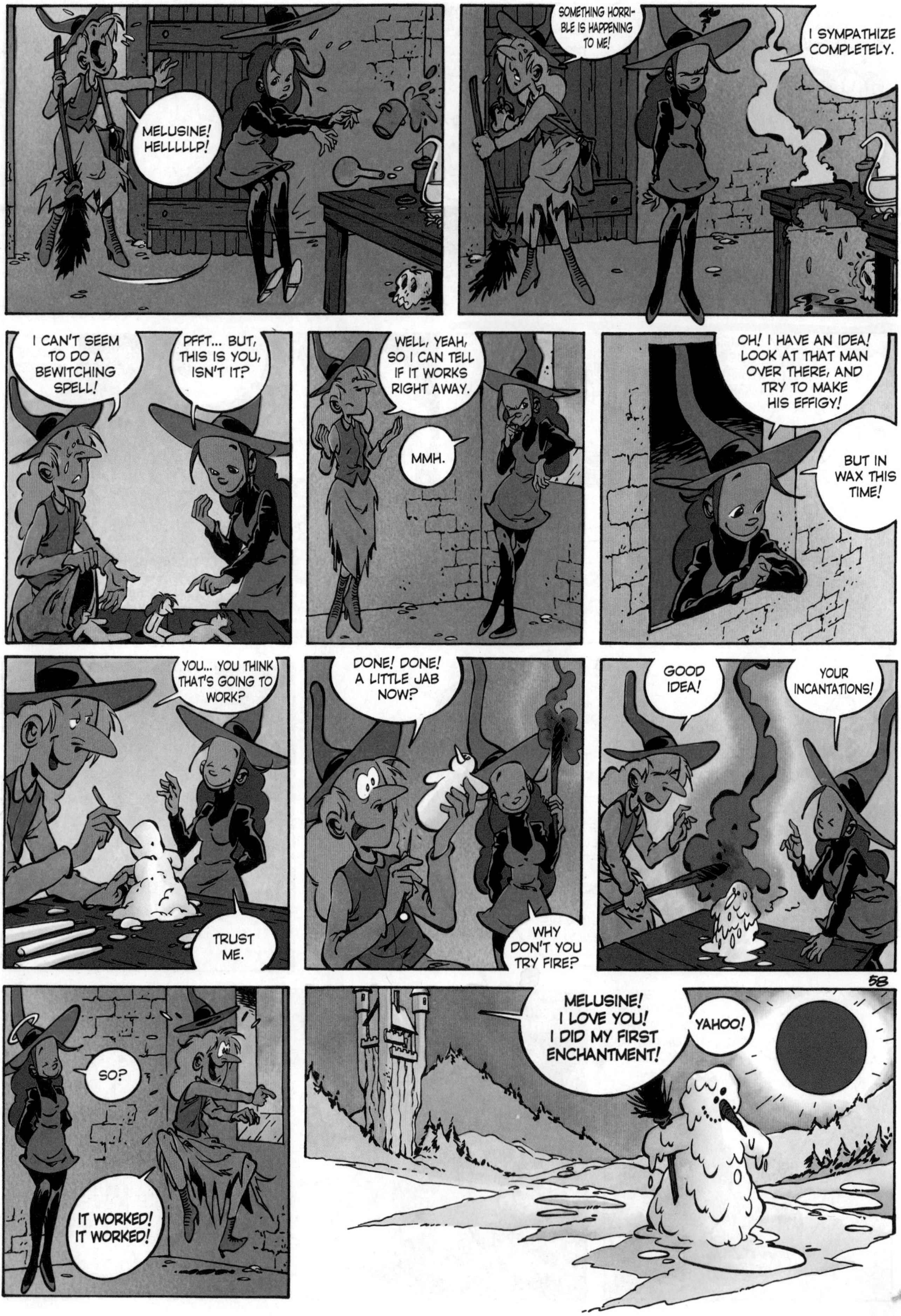
MELUSINE! HELLLLLLP!
SOMETHING HORRIBLE IS HAPPENING TO ME!
I SYMPATHIZE COMPLETELY.
I CAN'T SEEM TO DO A BEWITCHING SPELL!
PFFT... BUT, THIS IS YOU, ISN'T IT?
WELL, YEAH, SO I CAN TELL IF IT WORKS RIGHT AWAY.
MMH.
OH! I HAVE AN IDEA! LOOK AT THAT MAN OVER THERE, AND TRY TO MAKE HIS EFFIGY!
BUT IN WAX THIS TIME!
YOU... YOU THINK THAT'S GOING TO WORK?
TRUST ME.
DONE! DONE! A LITTLE JAB NOW?
WHY DON'T YOU TRY FIRE?
GOOD IDEA!
YOUR INCANTATIONS!
58
SO?
IT WORKED! IT WORKED!
MELUSINE! I LOVE YOU! I DID MY FIRST ENCHANTMENT!
YAHOO!

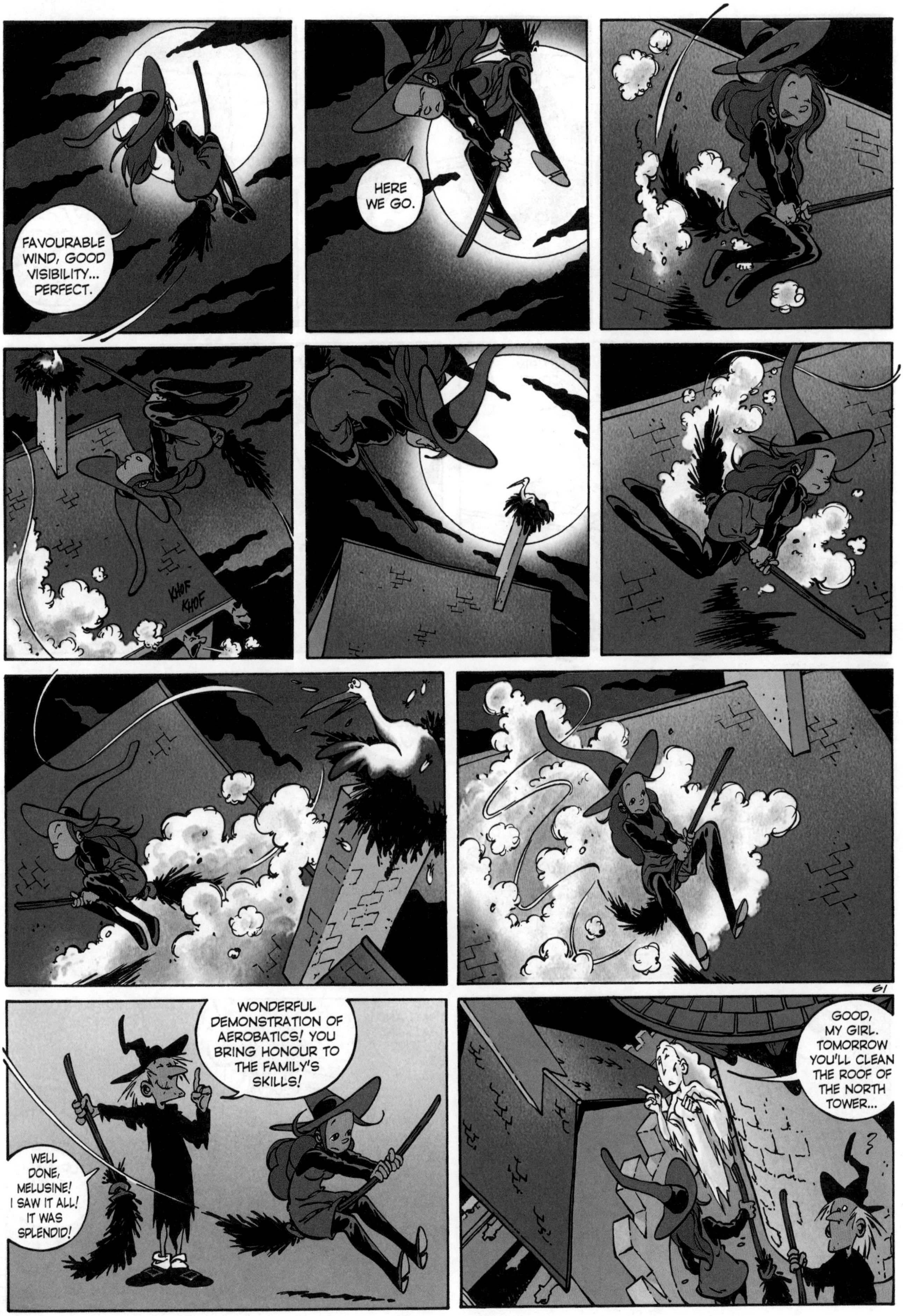
FAVOURABLE WIND, GOOD VISIBILITY... PERFECT.
HERE WE GO.
KHOF KHOF
WONDERFUL DEMONSTRATION OF AEROBATICS! YOU BRING HONOUR TO THE FAMILY'S SKILLS!
WELL DONE, MELUSINE! I SAW IT ALL! IT WAS SPLENDID!
GOOD, MY GIRL. TOMORROW YOU'LL CLEAN THE ROOF OF THE NORTH TOWER...
?

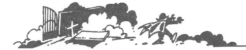

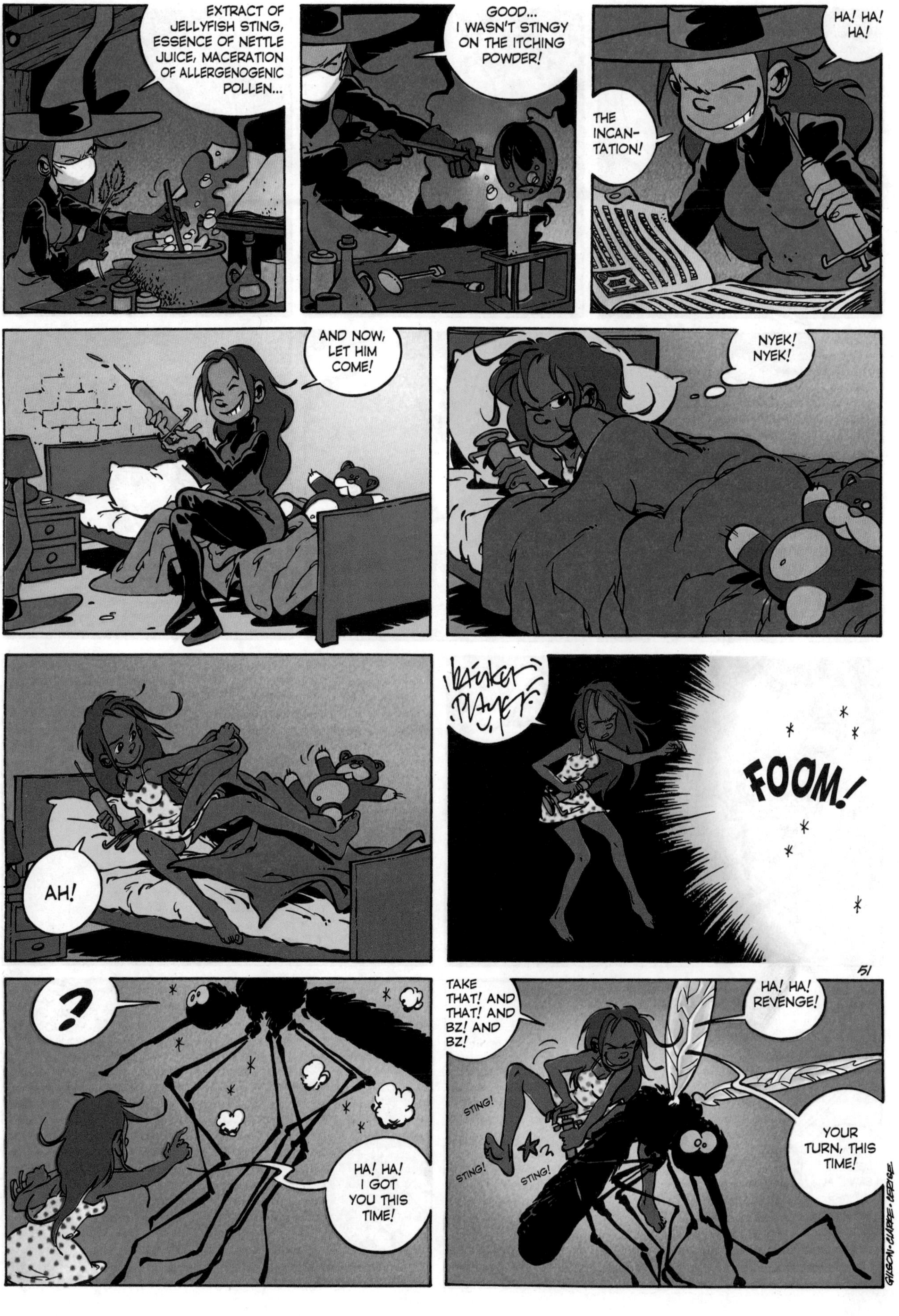
EXTRACT OF JELLYFISH STING, ESSENCE OF NETTLE JUICE, MACERATION OF ALLERGENOGENIC POLLEN...
GOOD... I WASN'T STINGY ON THE ITCHING POWDER!
HA! HA! HA!
THE INCANTATION!
AND NOW, LET HIM COME!
NYEK! NYEK!
AH!
FOOM!
?
HA! HA! I GOT YOU THIS TIME!
TAKE THAT! AND THAT! AND BZ! AND BZ!
HA! HA! REVENGE!
STING!
STING!
STING!
YOUR TURN, THIS TIME!

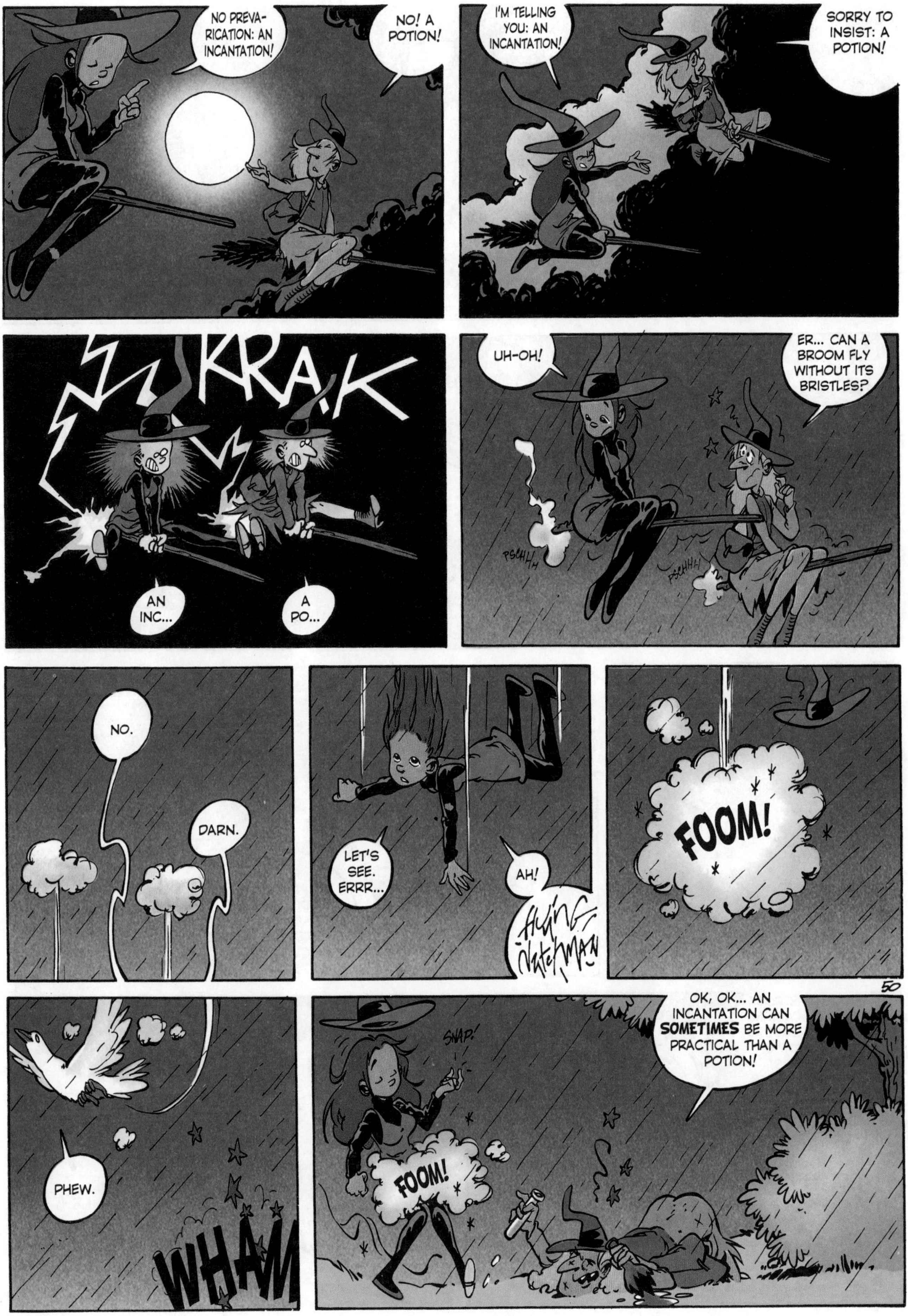
NO PREVA-RICATION: AN INCANTATION!
NO! A POTION!
I'M TELLING YOU: AN INCANTATION!
SORRY TO INSIST: A POTION!
KRAAK
AN INC...
A PO...
UH-OH!
ER... CAN A BROOM FLY WITHOUT ITS BRISTLES?
NO.
DARN.
LET'S SEE. ERRR...
AH!
FOOM!
PHEW.
WHAM
SNAP!
OK, OK... AN INCANTATION CAN **SOMETIMES** BE MORE PRACTICAL THAN A POTION!
FOOM!

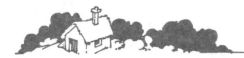

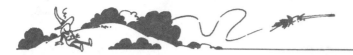

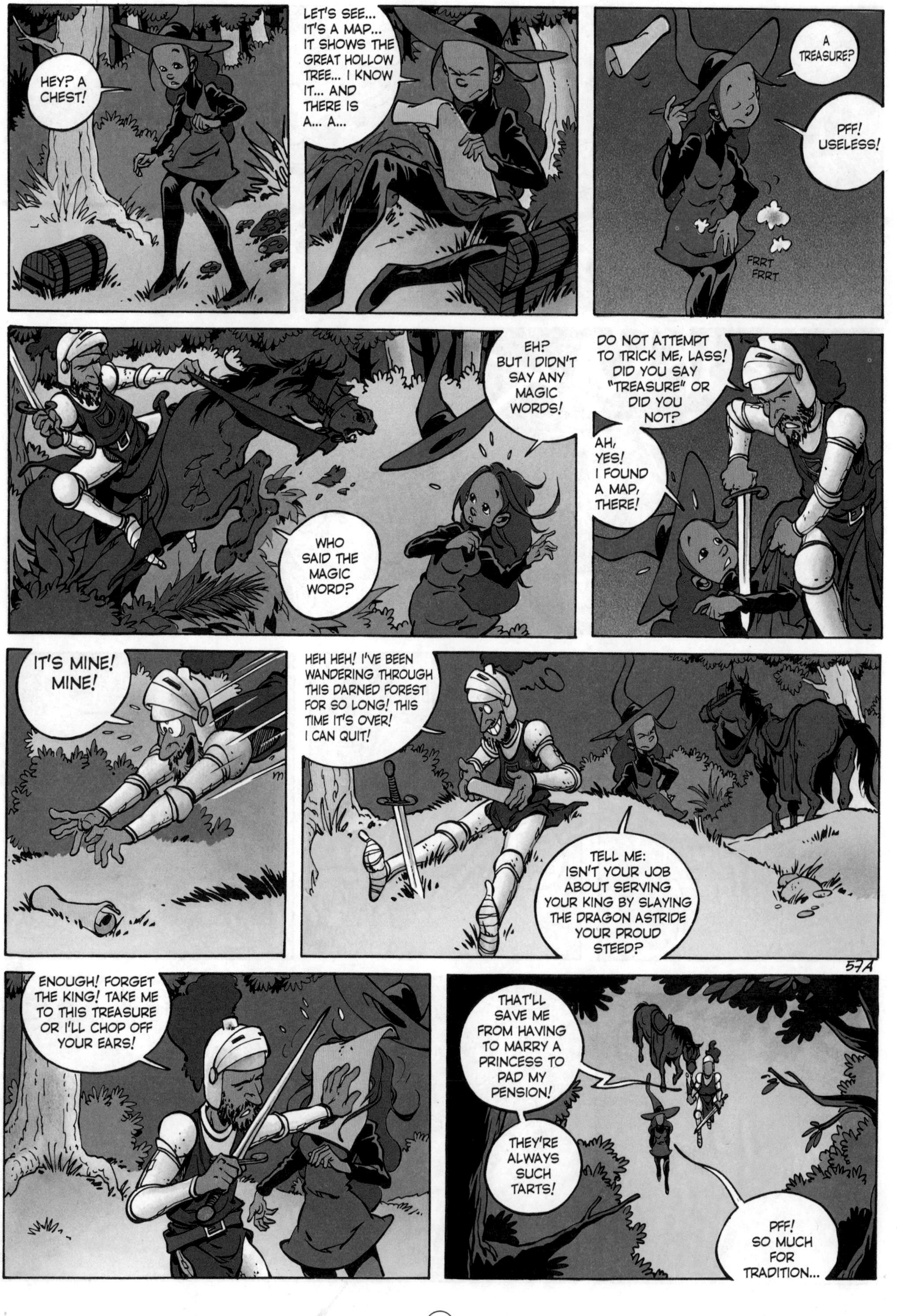
HEY? A CHEST!
LET'S SEE... IT'S A MAP... IT SHOWS THE GREAT HOLLOW TREE... I KNOW IT... AND THERE IS A... A...
A TREASURE?
PFF! USELESS!
FRRT FRRT
EH? BUT I DIDN'T SAY ANY MAGIC WORDS!
WHO SAID THE MAGIC WORD?
DO NOT ATTEMPT TO TRICK ME, LASS! DID YOU SAY "TREASURE" OR DID YOU NOT?
AH, YES! I FOUND A MAP, THERE!
IT'S MINE! MINE!
HEH HEH! I'VE BEEN WANDERING THROUGH THIS DARNED FOREST FOR SO LONG! THIS TIME IT'S OVER! I CAN QUIT!
TELL ME: ISN'T YOUR JOB ABOUT SERVING YOUR KING BY SLAYING THE DRAGON ASTRIDE YOUR PROUD STEED?
57A
ENOUGH! FORGET THE KING! TAKE ME TO THIS TREASURE OR I'LL CHOP OFF YOUR EARS!
THAT'LL SAVE ME FROM HAVING TO MARRY A PRINCESS TO PAD MY PENSION!
THEY'RE ALWAYS SUCH TARTS!
PFF! SO MUCH FOR TRADITION...

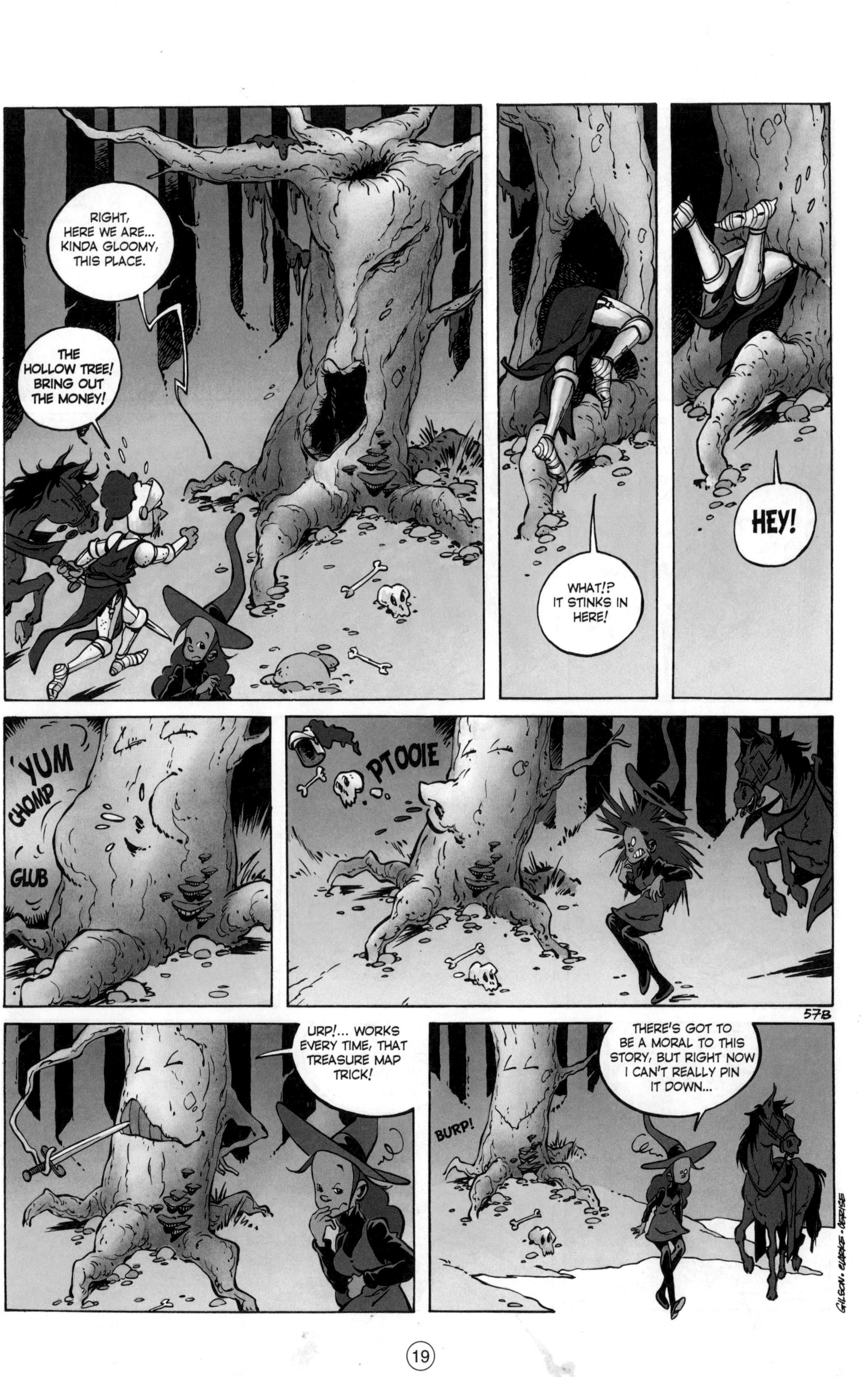
RIGHT, HERE WE ARE... KINDA GLOOMY, THIS PLACE.
THE HOLLOW TREE! BRING OUT THE MONEY!
WHAT!? IT STINKS IN HERE!
HEY!
YUM
CHOMP
GLUB
PTOOIE
57B
URP!... WORKS EVERY TIME, THAT TREASURE MAP TRICK!
THERE'S GOT TO BE A MORAL TO THIS STORY, BUT RIGHT NOW I CAN'T REALLY PIN IT DOWN...
BURP!

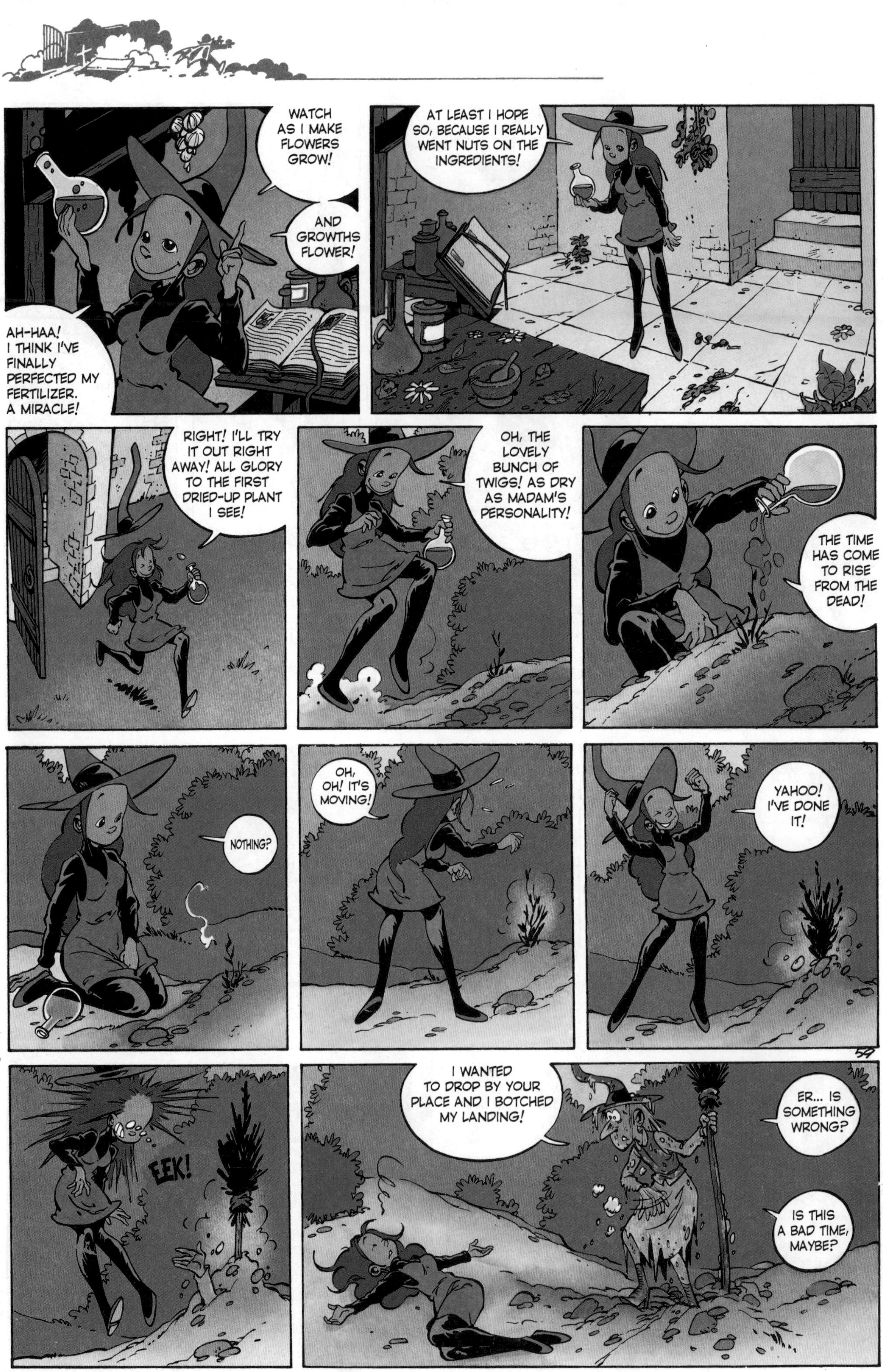
WATCH AS I MAKE FLOWERS GROW!
AND GROWTHS FLOWER!
AH-HAA! I THINK I'VE FINALLY PERFECTED MY FERTILIZER. A MIRACLE!
AT LEAST I HOPE SO, BECAUSE I REALLY WENT NUTS ON THE INGREDIENTS!
RIGHT! I'LL TRY IT OUT RIGHT AWAY! ALL GLORY TO THE FIRST DRIED-UP PLANT I SEE!
OH, THE LOVELY BUNCH OF TWIGS! AS DRY AS MADAM'S PERSONALITY!
THE TIME HAS COME TO RISE FROM THE DEAD!
NOTHING?
OH, OH! IT'S MOVING!
YAHOO! I'VE DONE IT!
EEK!
I WANTED TO DROP BY YOUR PLACE AND I BOTCHED MY LANDING!
ER... IS SOMETHING WRONG?
IS THIS A BAD TIME, MAYBE?

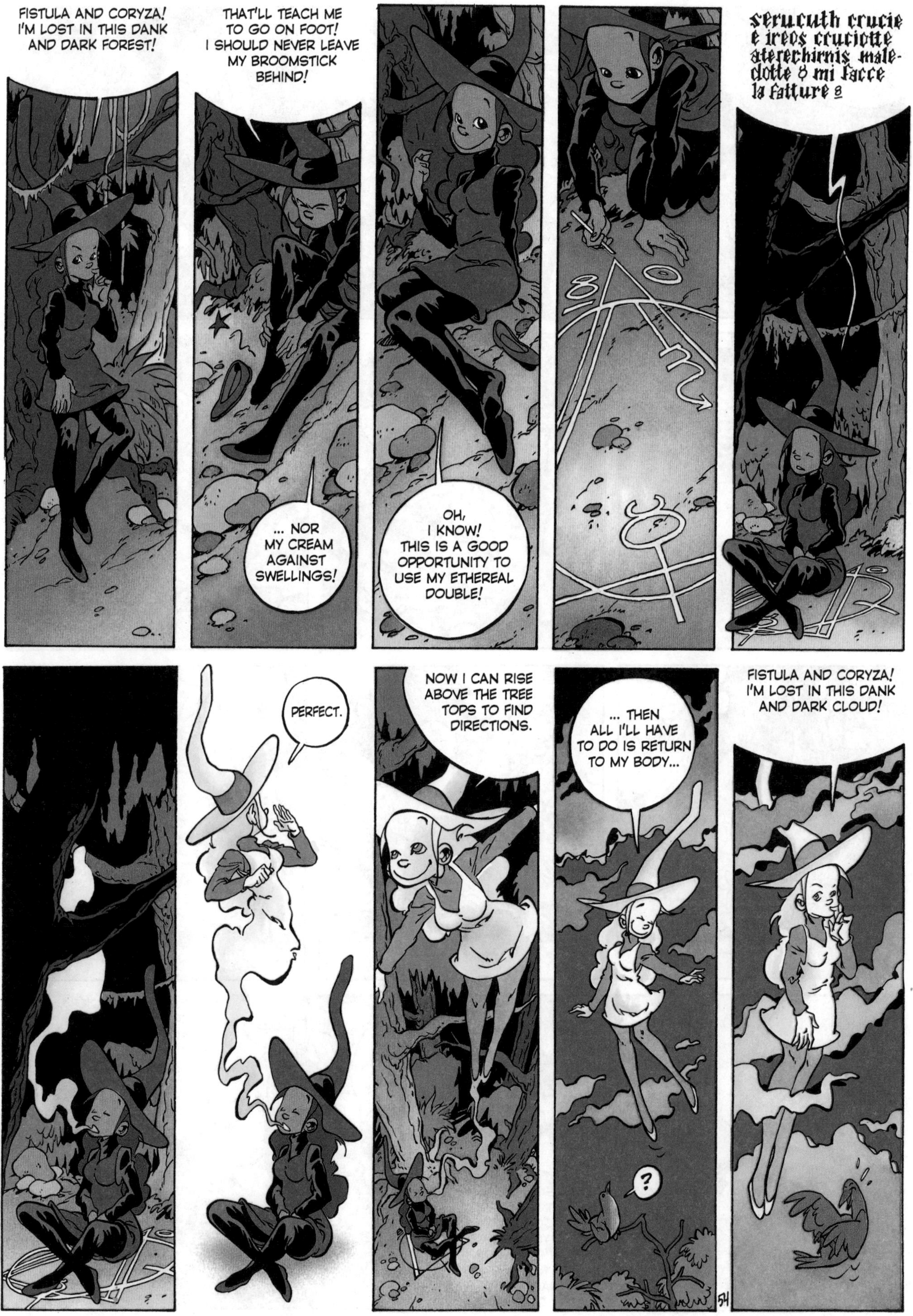
FISTULA AND CORYZA! I'M LOST IN THIS DANK AND DARK FOREST!
THAT'LL TEACH ME TO GO ON FOOT! I SHOULD NEVER LEAVE MY BROOMSTICK BEHIND!
... NOR MY CREAM AGAINST SWELLINGS!
OH, I KNOW! THIS IS A GOOD OPPORTUNITY TO USE MY ETHEREAL DOUBLE!
serucuth crucie e ireos cruciotte aterechirnis male-clotte 8 mi facce la fatture 8
PERFECT.
NOW I CAN RISE ABOVE THE TREE TOPS TO FIND DIRECTIONS.
... THEN ALL I'LL HAVE TO DO IS RETURN TO MY BODY...
?
FISTULA AND CORYZA! I'M LOST IN THIS DANK AND DARK CLOUD!

LOOK AT THIS, AUNTIE. I'LL SHOW YOU SOMETHING...

A NICE LITTLE PUSTULOUS TOAD? GOOD IDEA! I FANCIED A VISCOUS SOUP.

NO, WAIT!

URESUB!

AND THERE YOU GO!

63

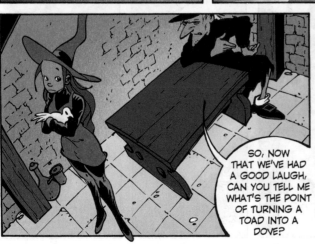

SO, NOW THAT WE'VE HAD A GOOD LAUGH, CAN YOU TELL ME WHAT'S THE POINT OF TURNING A TOAD INTO A DOVE?

WELL... JUST FOR PURE AND SIMPLE BEAUTY, TO PLEASE THE EYES, THE POESY... NO?

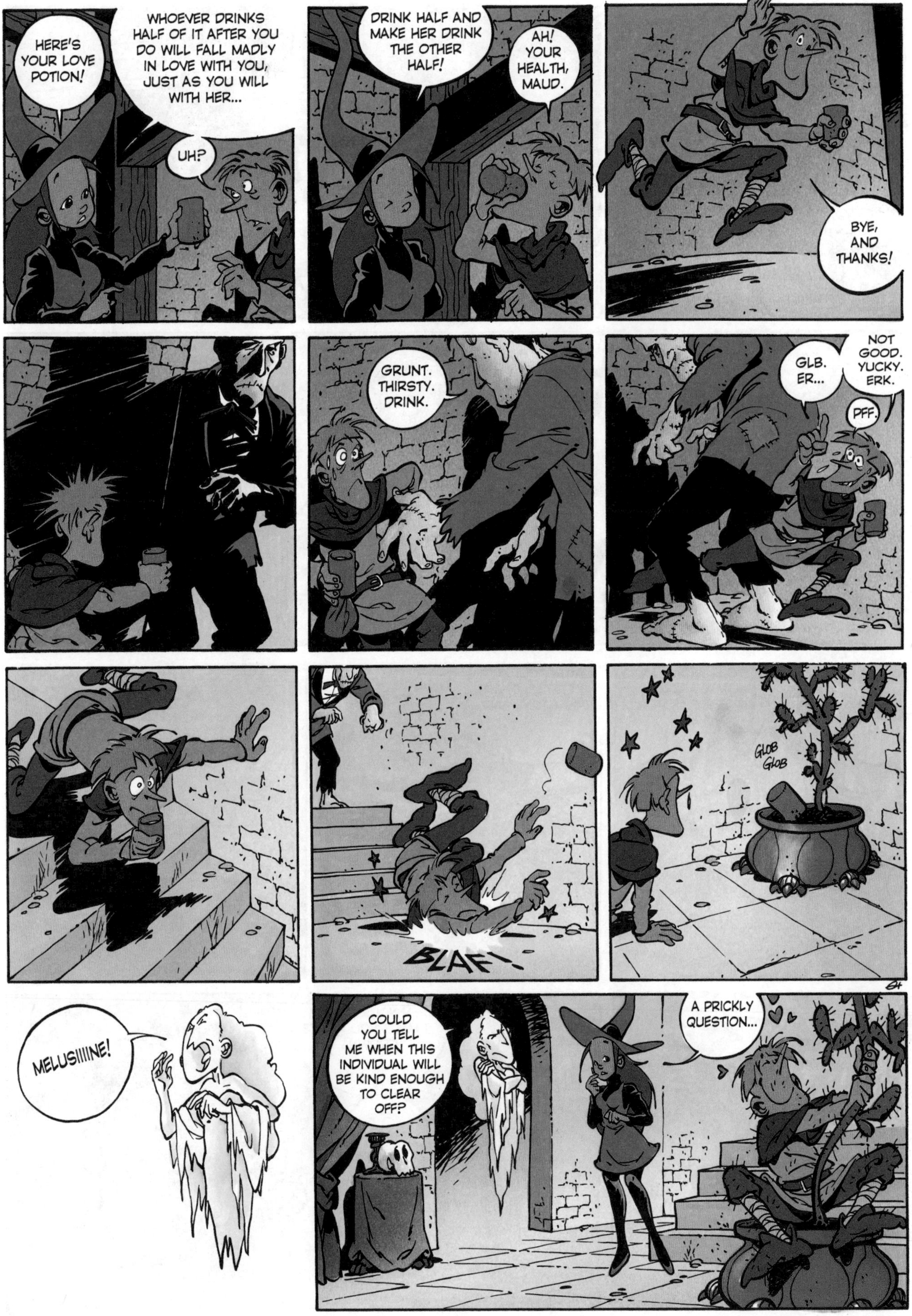
HERE'S YOUR LOVE POTION!
WHOEVER DRINKS HALF OF IT AFTER YOU DO WILL FALL MADLY IN LOVE WITH YOU, JUST AS YOU WILL WITH HER...
UH?
DRINK HALF AND MAKE HER DRINK THE OTHER HALF!
AH! YOUR HEALTH, MAUD.
BYE, AND THANKS!
GRUNT. THIRSTY. DRINK.
GLB. ER...
NOT GOOD. YUCKY. ERK.
PFF.
BLAF!
GLOB GLOB
MELUSIIIINE!
COULD YOU TELL ME WHEN THIS INDIVIDUAL WILL BE KIND ENOUGH TO CLEAR OFF?
A PRICKLY QUESTION...

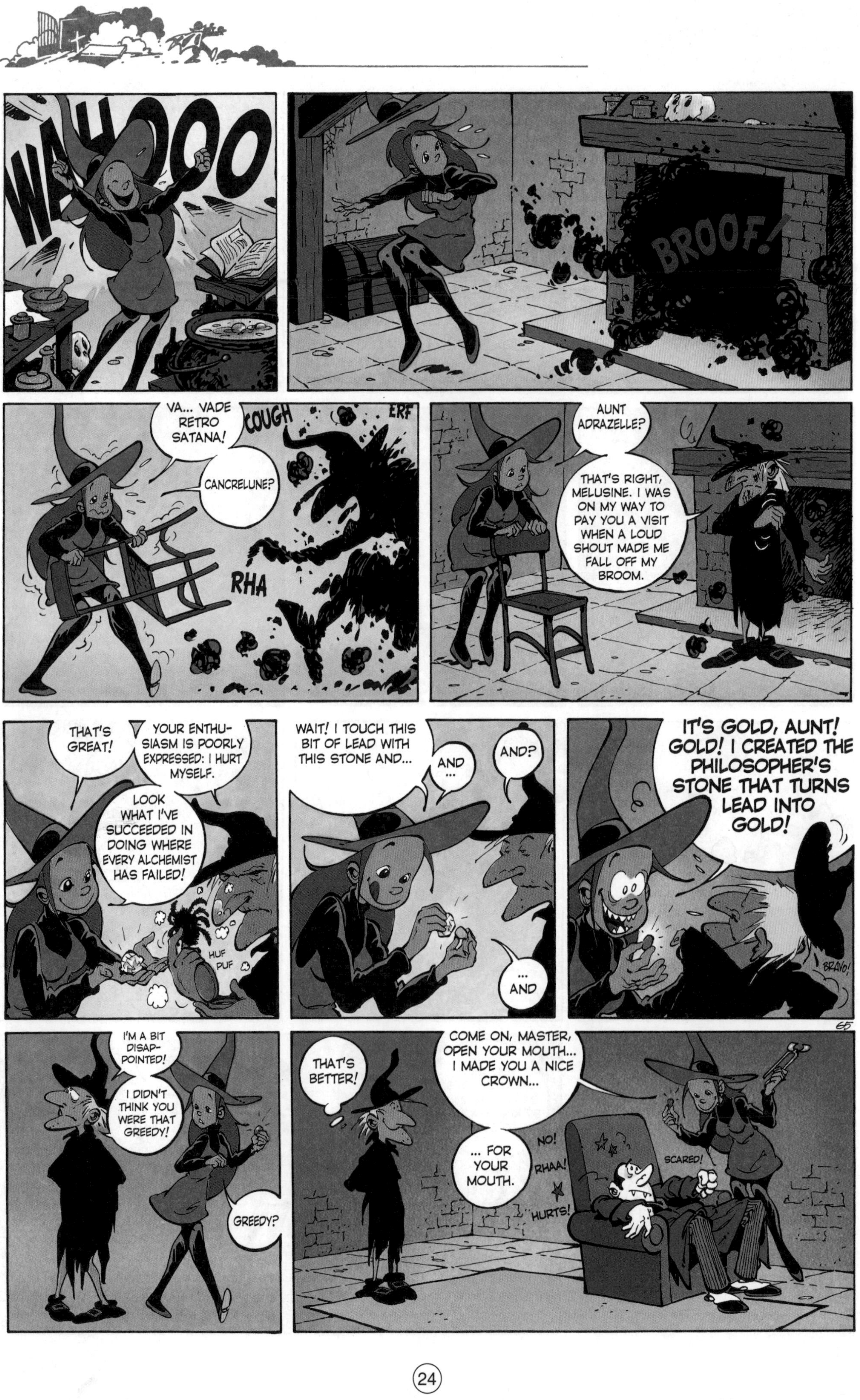
WAHOOO
BROOF!
VA... VADE RETRO SATANA!
COUGH
ERF
CANCRELUNE?
RHA
AUNT ADRAZELLE?
THAT'S RIGHT, MELUSINE. I WAS ON MY WAY TO PAY YOU A VISIT WHEN A LOUD SHOUT MADE ME FALL OFF MY BROOM.
THAT'S GREAT!
YOUR ENTHUSIASM IS POORLY EXPRESSED: I HURT MYSELF.
LOOK WHAT I'VE SUCCEEDED IN DOING WHERE EVERY ALCHEMIST HAS FAILED!
HUF PUF
WAIT! I TOUCH THIS BIT OF LEAD WITH THIS STONE AND...
AND ...
AND?
... AND
IT'S GOLD, AUNT! GOLD! I CREATED THE PHILOSOPHER'S STONE THAT TURNS LEAD INTO GOLD!
BRAVO!
I'M A BIT DISAPPOINTED!
I DIDN'T THINK YOU WERE THAT GREEDY!
GREEDY?
THAT'S BETTER!
COME ON, MASTER, OPEN YOUR MOUTH... I MADE YOU A NICE CROWN...
... FOR YOUR MOUTH.
NO!
RHAA!
HURTS!
SCARED!

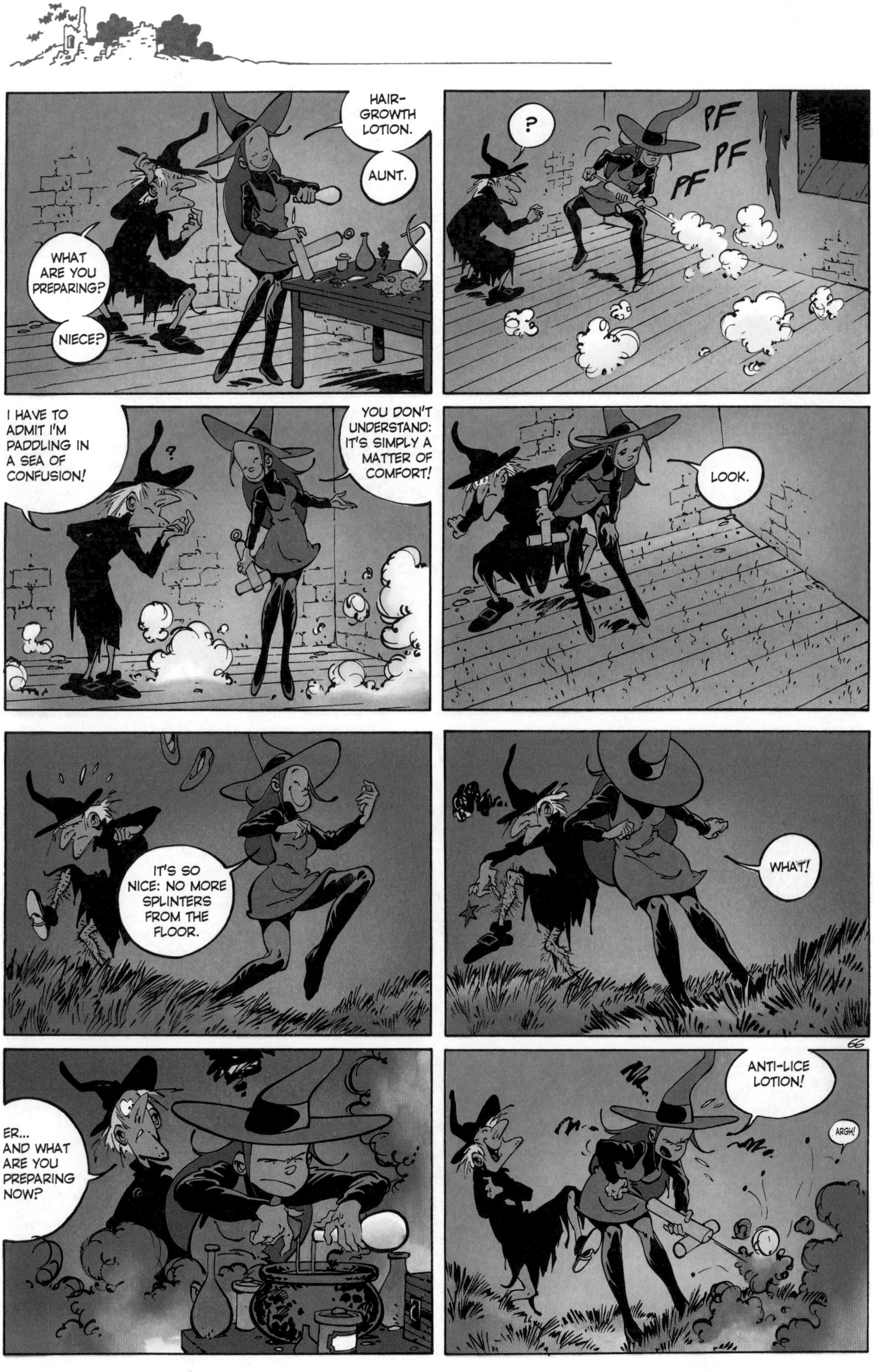
WHAT ARE YOU PREPARING?
NIECE?
HAIR-GROWTH LOTION.
AUNT.
?
PF PF PF
I HAVE TO ADMIT I'M PADDLING IN A SEA OF CONFUSION!
?
YOU DON'T UNDERSTAND: IT'S SIMPLY A MATTER OF COMFORT!
LOOK.
IT'S SO NICE: NO MORE SPLINTERS FROM THE FLOOR.
WHAT!
ER... AND WHAT ARE YOU PREPARING NOW?
ANTI-LICE LOTION!
ARGH!

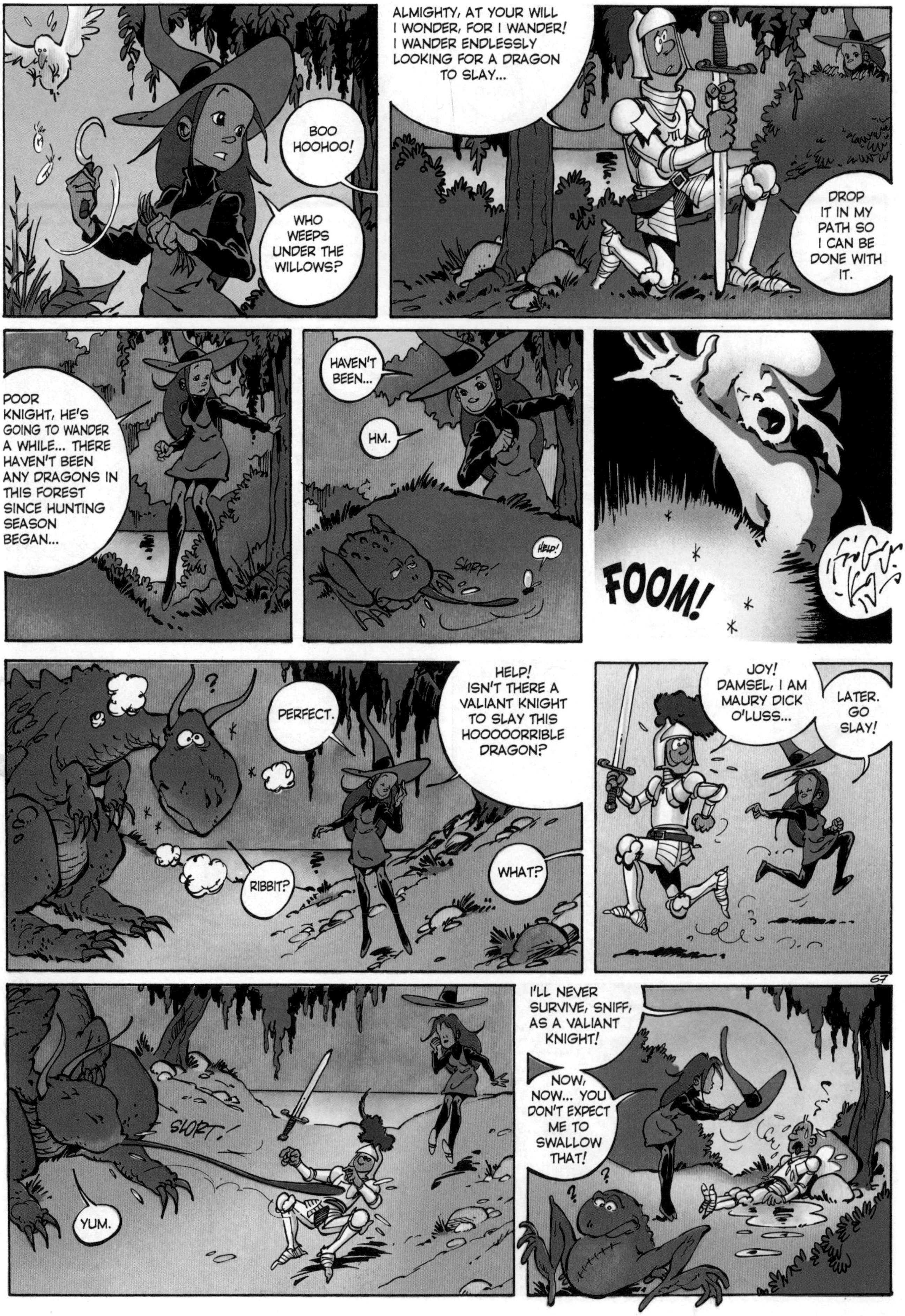

BOO HOOHOO!
WHO WEEPS UNDER THE WILLOWS?
ALMIGHTY, AT YOUR WILL I WONDER, FOR I WANDER! I WANDER ENDLESSLY LOOKING FOR A DRAGON TO SLAY...
DROP IT IN MY PATH SO I CAN BE DONE WITH IT.
POOR KNIGHT, HE'S GOING TO WANDER A WHILE... THERE HAVEN'T BEEN ANY DRAGONS IN THIS FOREST SINCE HUNTING SEASON BEGAN...
HAVEN'T BEEN...
HM.
SLORP!
HELP!
FOOM!
PERFECT.
RIBBIT?
HELP! ISN'T THERE A VALIANT KNIGHT TO SLAY THIS HOOOOORRIBLE DRAGON?
WHAT?
JOY! DAMSEL, I AM MAURY DICK O'LUSS...
LATER. GO SLAY!
SLORT!
YUM.
I'LL NEVER SURVIVE, SNIFF, AS A VALIANT KNIGHT!
NOW, NOW... YOU DON'T EXPECT ME TO SWALLOW THAT!

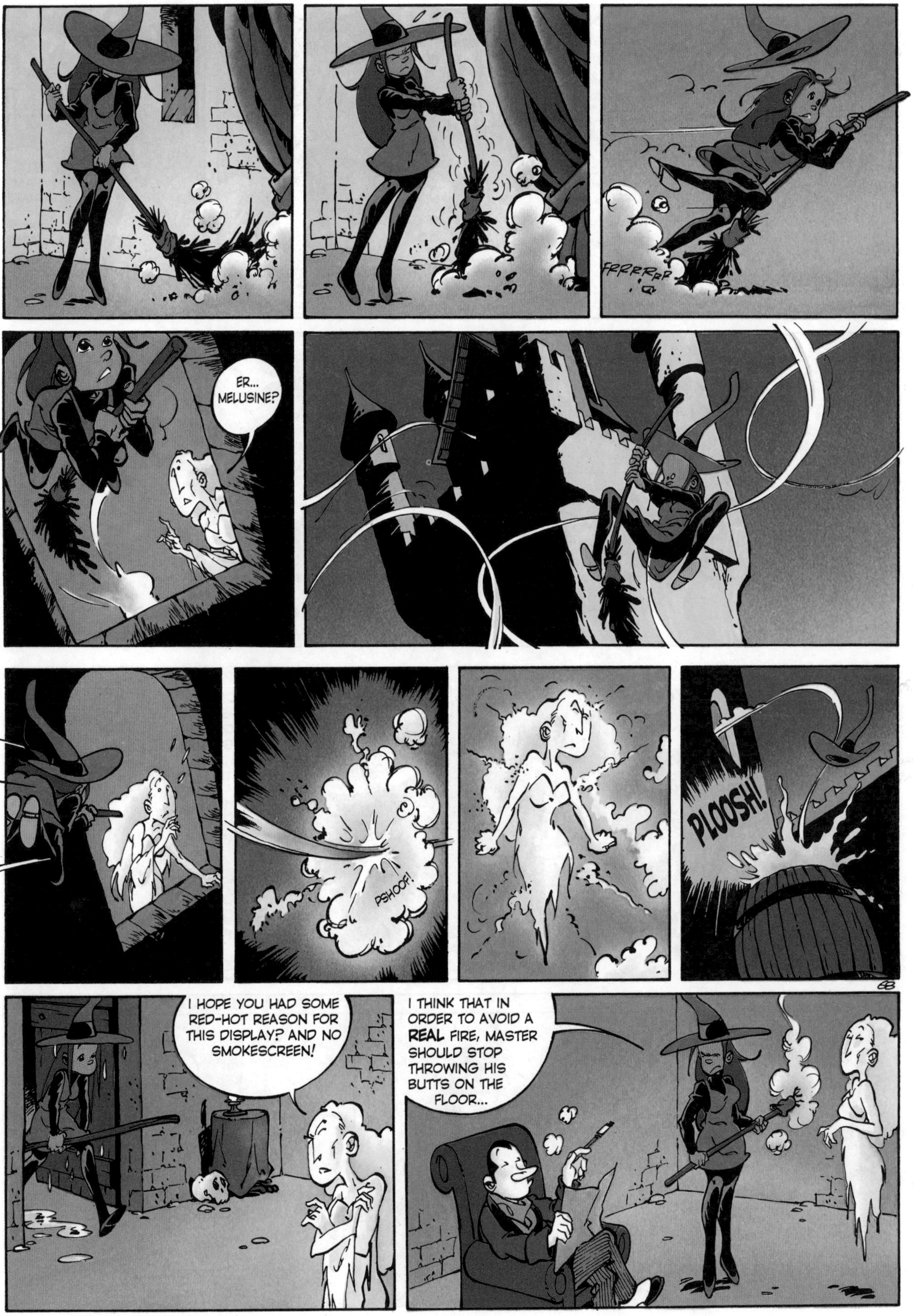
FRRRRRP
ER... MELUSINE?
PSHOOF!
PLOOSH!
I HOPE YOU HAD SOME RED-HOT REASON FOR THIS DISPLAY? AND NO SMOKESCREEN!
I THINK THAT IN ORDER TO AVOID A REAL FIRE, MASTER SHOULD STOP THROWING HIS BUTTS ON THE FLOOR...

MELUSINE, HE'S TERRORISING US!

... AND HE'S HORRIBLE!

URK!

I'LL CHECK IT OUT.

IT'S WONDERFUL THAT YOU'RE NOT AFRAID.

BUT I AM AFRAID!

PHLEBITIS AND CORYZA!

ROAR!

FROOSSHHHH!

:ràjùéli:

FOOM!

OHH... YOU JUST HAVE A COLD, DON'T YOU? DO YOU REALISE YOU'RE TERRORISING THE WHOLE NEIGHBOURHOOD?

SNURFL!

COME ON, THEN. I'LL TAKE YOU HOME TO REST, AND YOU'LL FEEL BETTER...

AA... AA... AA...

69

CHOOOOOO

?

... IN NO TIME...

SNIRF

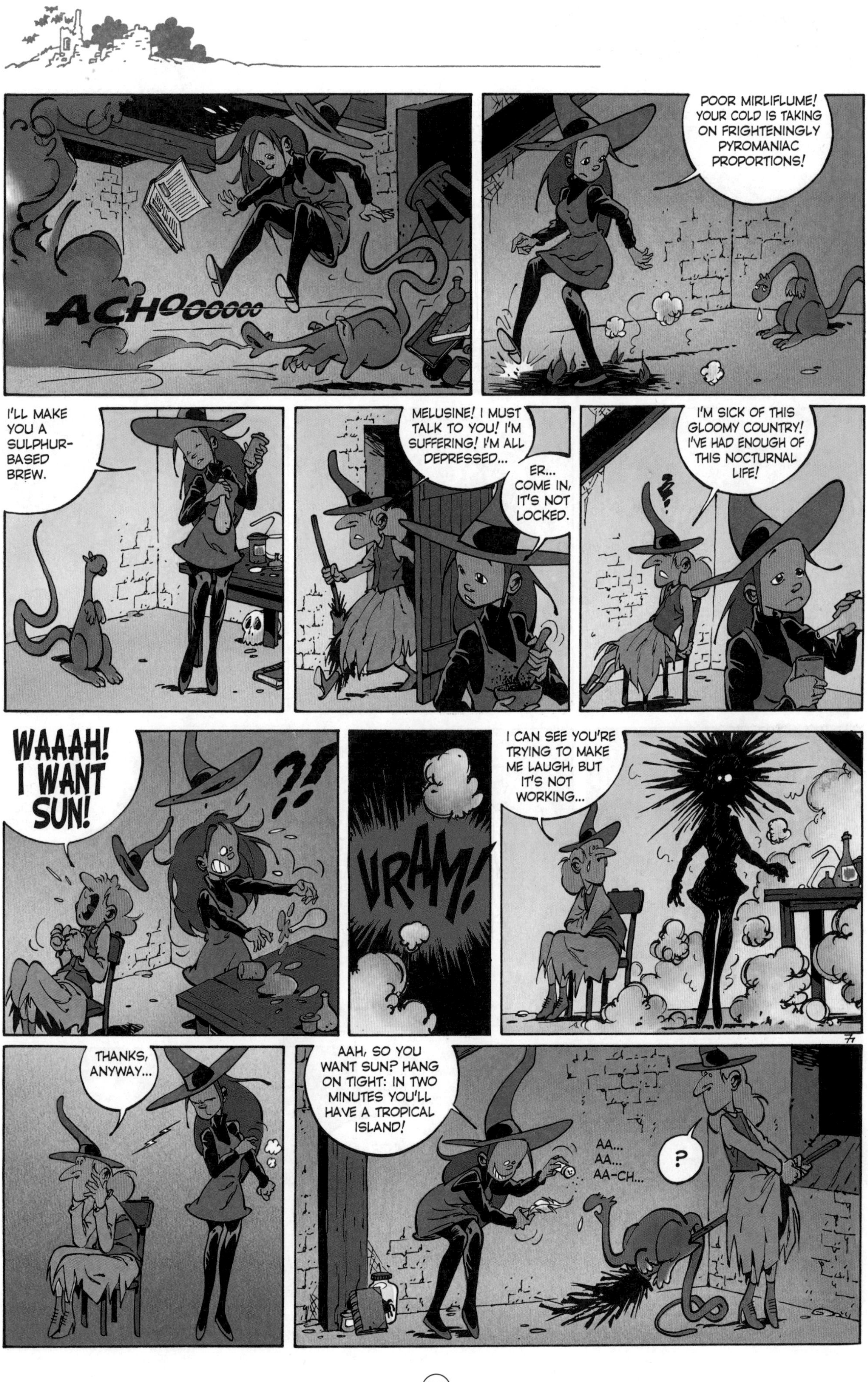
ACHOOOOOO
POOR MIRLIFLUME! YOUR COLD IS TAKING ON FRIGHTENINGLY PYROMANIAC PROPORTIONS!
I'LL MAKE YOU A SULPHUR-BASED BREW.
MELUSINE! I MUST TALK TO YOU! I'M SUFFERING! I'M ALL DEPRESSED...
ER... COME IN, IT'S NOT LOCKED.
I'M SICK OF THIS GLOOMY COUNTRY! I'VE HAD ENOUGH OF THIS NOCTURNAL LIFE!
WAAAH! I WANT SUN!
?!
VRAM!
I CAN SEE YOU'RE TRYING TO MAKE ME LAUGH, BUT IT'S NOT WORKING...
THANKS, ANYWAY...
AAH, SO YOU WANT SUN? HANG ON TIGHT: IN TWO MINUTES YOU'LL HAVE A TROPICAL ISLAND!
AA... AA... AA-CH...
?

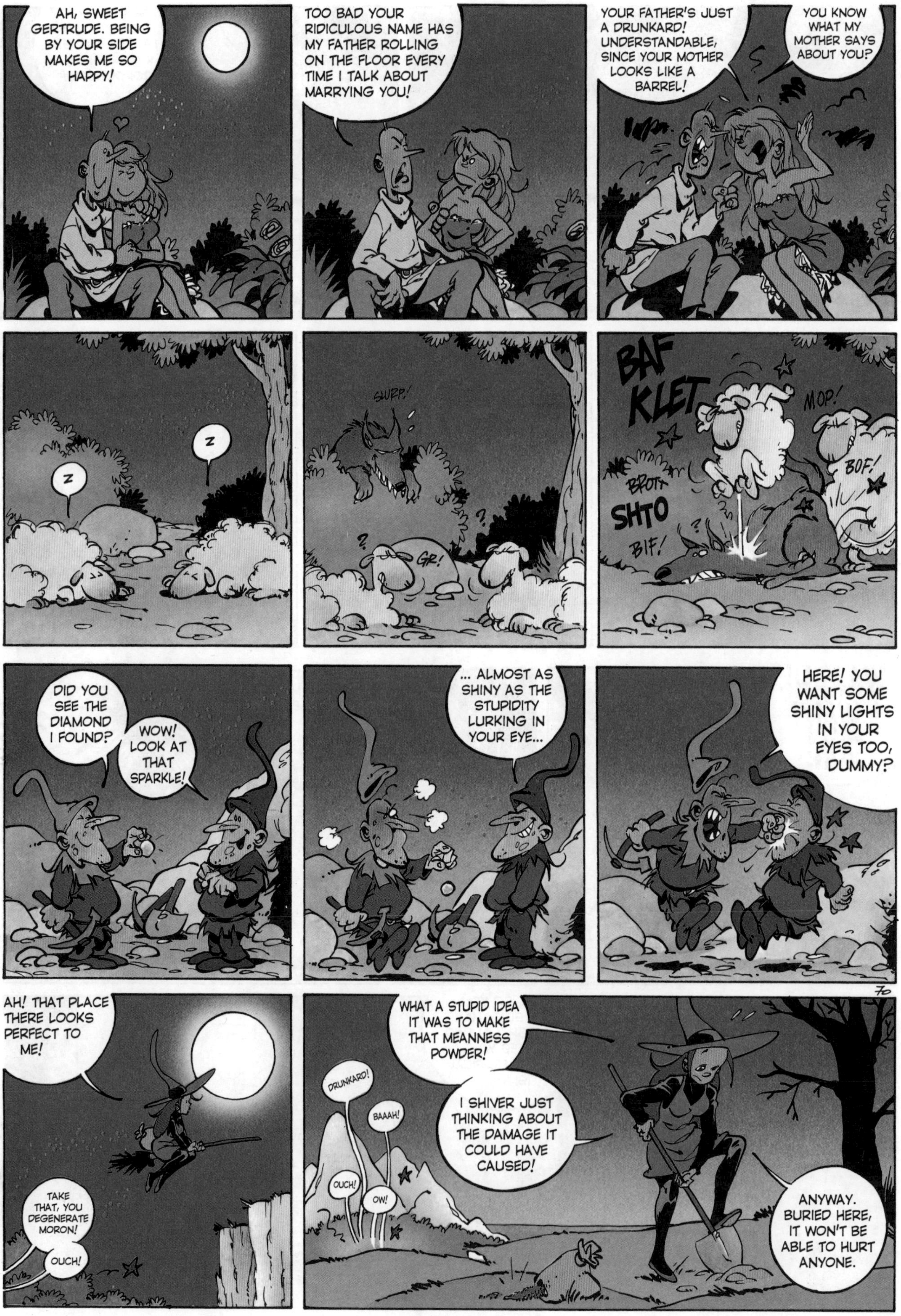
AH, SWEET GERTRUDE. BEING BY YOUR SIDE MAKES ME SO HAPPY!
TOO BAD YOUR RIDICULOUS NAME HAS MY FATHER ROLLING ON THE FLOOR EVERY TIME I TALK ABOUT MARRYING YOU!
YOUR FATHER'S JUST A DRUNKARD! UNDERSTANDABLE, SINCE YOUR MOTHER LOOKS LIKE A BARREL!
YOU KNOW WHAT MY MOTHER SAYS ABOUT YOU?
Z
Z
SLURP!
?
?
GR!
BAF
KLET
MOP!
BROTT
SHTO
BOF!
?
BIF!
DID YOU SEE THE DIAMOND I FOUND?
WOW! LOOK AT THAT SPARKLE!
... ALMOST AS SHINY AS THE STUPIDITY LURKING IN YOUR EYE...
HERE! YOU WANT SOME SHINY LIGHTS IN YOUR EYES TOO, DUMMY?
AH! THAT PLACE THERE LOOKS PERFECT TO ME!
TAKE THAT, YOU DEGENERATE MORON!
OUCH!
WHAT A STUPID IDEA IT WAS TO MAKE THAT MEANNESS POWDER!
DRUNKARD!
BAAAH!
I SHIVER JUST THINKING ABOUT THE DAMAGE IT COULD HAVE CAUSED!
OUCH!
OW!
ANYWAY. BURIED HERE, IT WON'T BE ABLE TO HURT ANYONE.

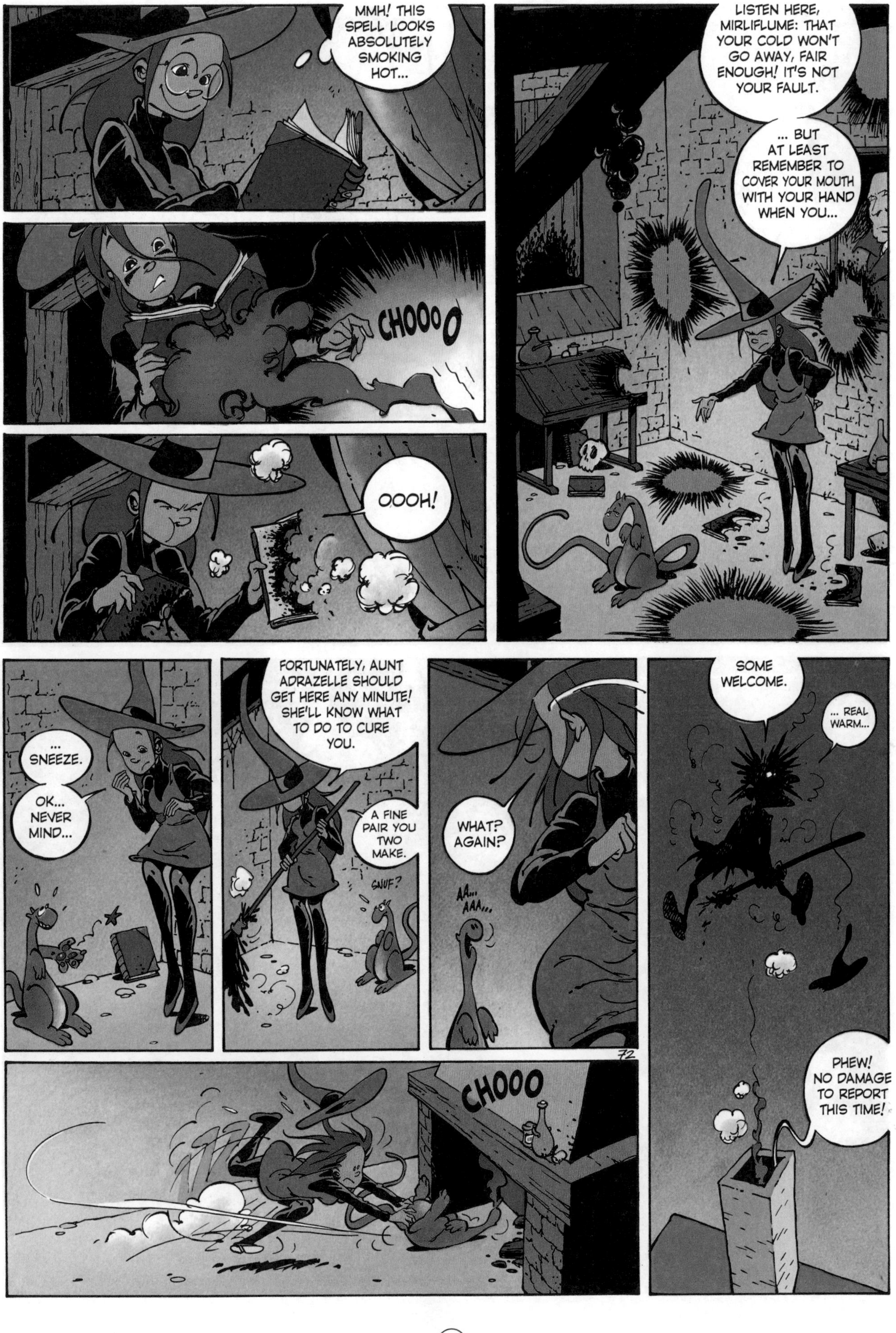
MMH! THIS SPELL LOOKS ABSOLUTELY SMOKING HOT...
CHOOOO
OOOH!
LISTEN HERE, MIRLIFLUME: THAT YOUR COLD WON'T GO AWAY, FAIR ENOUGH! IT'S NOT YOUR FAULT.
... BUT AT LEAST REMEMBER TO COVER YOUR MOUTH WITH YOUR HAND WHEN YOU...
... SNEEZE.
OK... NEVER MIND...
FORTUNATELY, AUNT ADRAZELLE SHOULD GET HERE ANY MINUTE! SHE'LL KNOW WHAT TO DO TO CURE YOU.
A FINE PAIR YOU TWO MAKE.
SNUF?
WHAT? AGAIN?
AA... AAA...
SOME WELCOME.
... REAL WARM...
CHOOO
PHEW! NO DAMAGE TO REPORT THIS TIME!

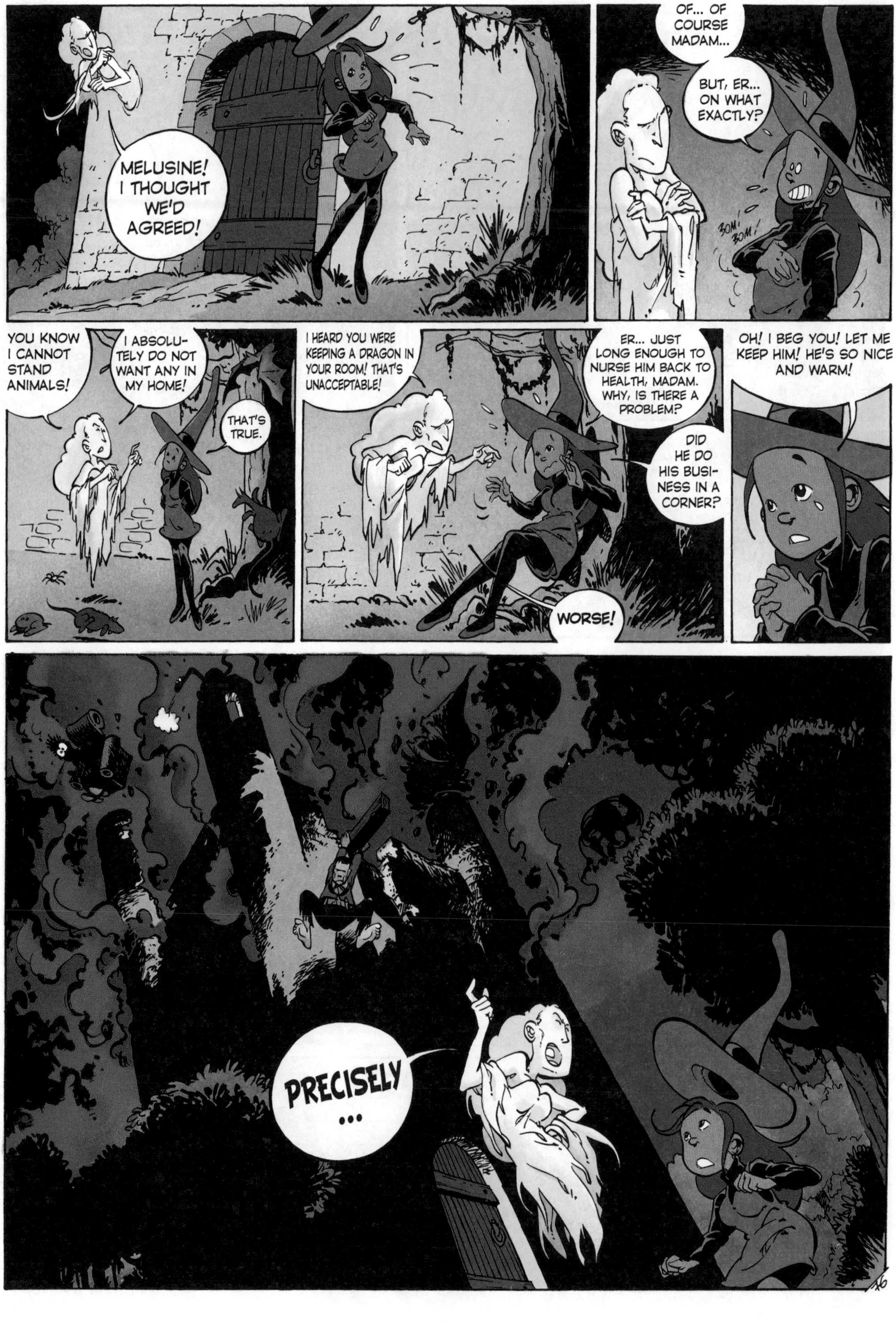
MELUSINE! I THOUGHT WE'D AGREED!
OF... OF COURSE MADAM...
BUT, ER... ON WHAT EXACTLY?
BOM! BOM!
YOU KNOW I CANNOT STAND ANIMALS!
I ABSOLUTELY DO NOT WANT ANY IN MY HOME!
THAT'S TRUE.
I HEARD YOU WERE KEEPING A DRAGON IN YOUR ROOM! THAT'S UNACCEPTABLE!
ER... JUST LONG ENOUGH TO NURSE HIM BACK TO HEALTH, MADAM. WHY, IS THERE A PROBLEM?
DID HE DO HIS BUSINESS IN A CORNER?
WORSE!
OH! I BEG YOU! LET ME KEEP HIM! HE'S SO NICE AND WARM!
PRECISELY ...

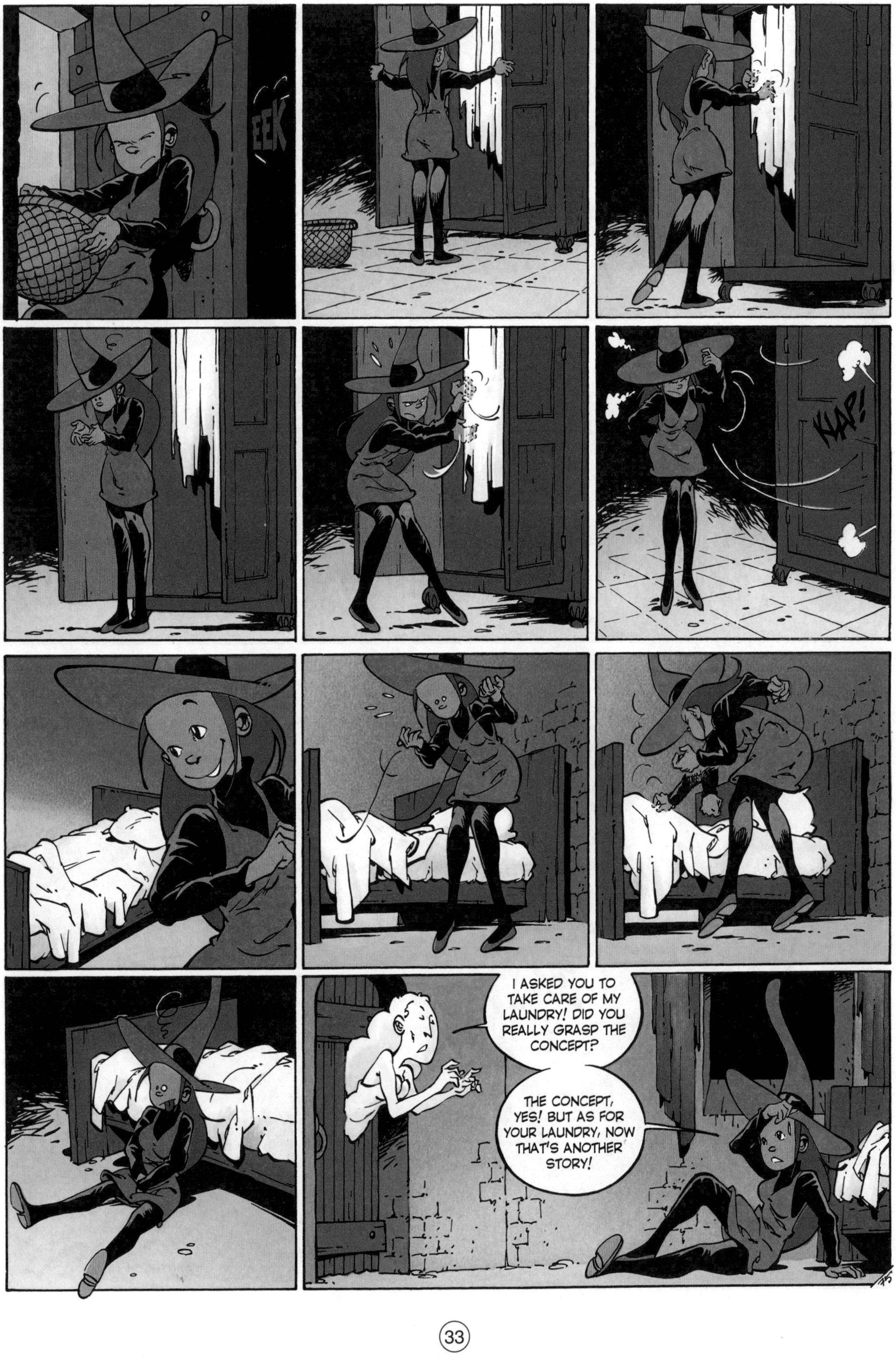
EEK
KLAP!
I ASKED YOU TO TAKE CARE OF MY LAUNDRY! DID YOU REALLY GRASP THE CONCEPT?
THE CONCEPT, YES! BUT AS FOR YOUR LAUNDRY, NOW THAT'S ANOTHER STORY!

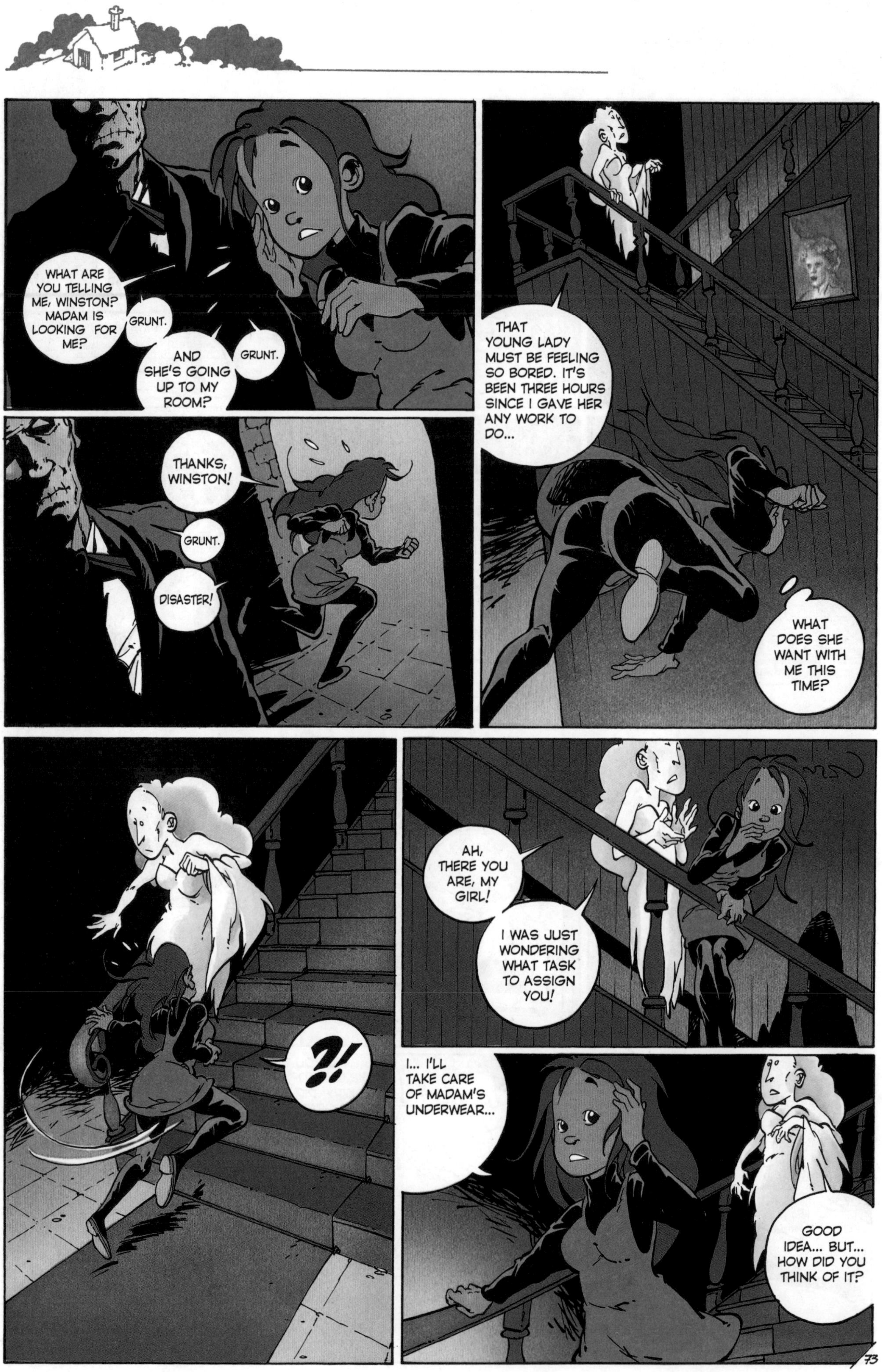
WHAT ARE YOU TELLING ME, WINSTON? MADAM IS LOOKING FOR ME?
GRUNT.
AND SHE'S GOING UP TO MY ROOM?
GRUNT.
THAT YOUNG LADY MUST BE FEELING SO BORED. IT'S BEEN THREE HOURS SINCE I GAVE HER ANY WORK TO DO...
THANKS, WINSTON!
GRUNT.
DISASTER!
WHAT DOES SHE WANT WITH ME THIS TIME?
?!
AH, THERE YOU ARE, MY GIRL!
I WAS JUST WONDERING WHAT TASK TO ASSIGN YOU!
I... I'LL TAKE CARE OF MADAM'S UNDERWEAR...
GOOD IDEA... BUT... HOW DID YOU THINK OF IT?
73

WHAT?! WHERE!?

GRUNT.

SPARE ME THE DETAILS, WINSTON! TELL ME WHERE!

GRUNT.

DERMATOSIS AND CORYZA!

I DIDN'T KNOW THERE WAS A TORTURE CHAMBER HERE!

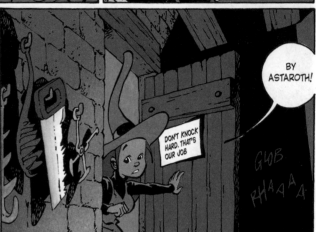

BY ASTAROTH!

DON'T KNOCK HARD. THAT'S OUR JOB

GLOB RHAAAA

WINSTON WAS RIGHT!

YOU WILL CONFESS, YOU SCOUNDREL!

AND DON'T SPEAK WITH YOUR MOUTH FULL!

GHURG GLORBL

ARE YOU OUT OF YOUR MIND?!

THIS IS MY BUCKET! IF YOU NEEDED IT, YOU SHOULD HAVE ASKED ME! FOR CRYING OUT LOUD!

ER... EXCUSE US...

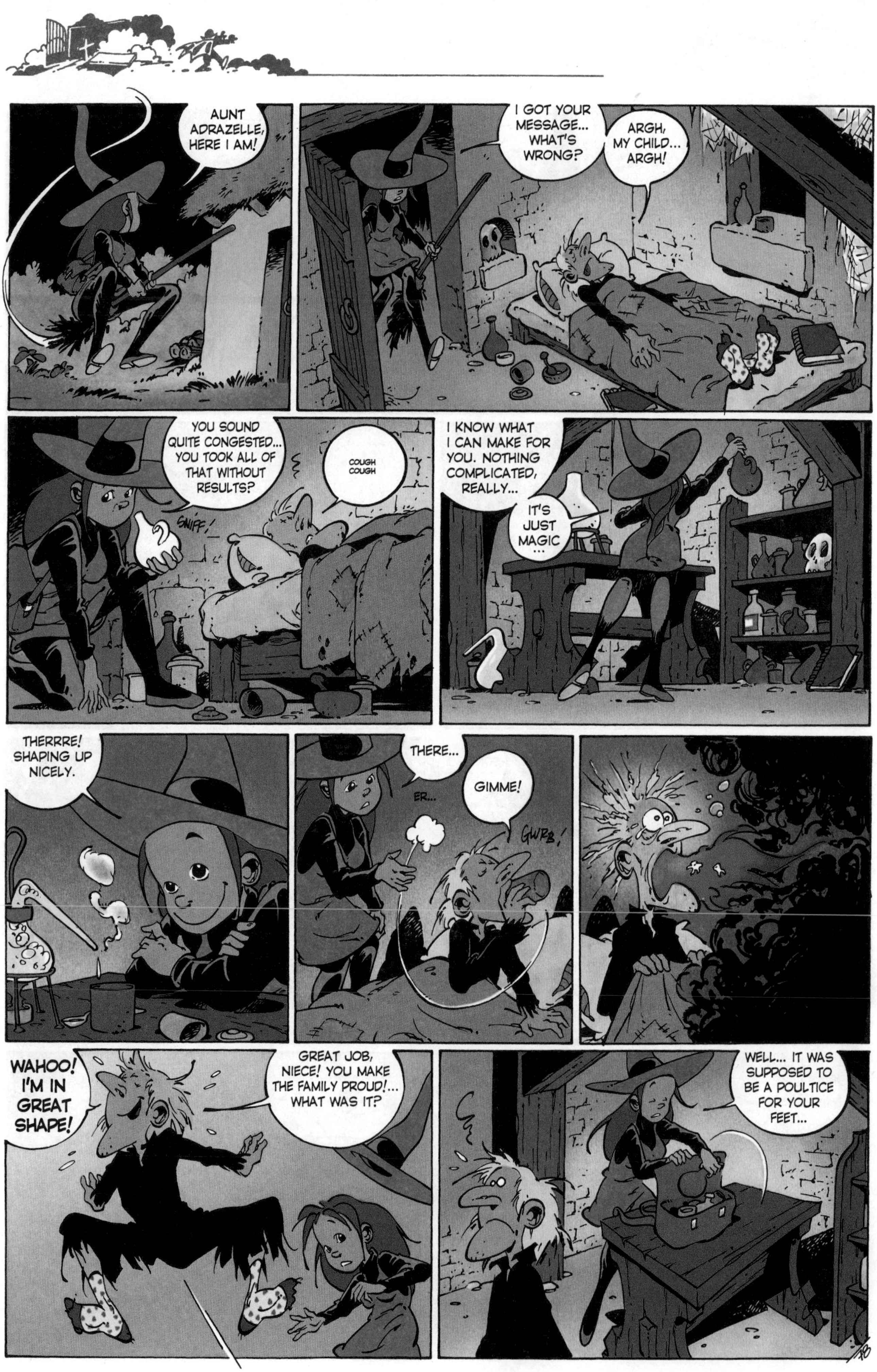
AUNT ADRAZELLE, HERE I AM!
I GOT YOUR MESSAGE... WHAT'S WRONG?
ARGH, MY CHILD... ARGH!
YOU SOUND QUITE CONGESTED... YOU TOOK ALL OF THAT WITHOUT RESULTS?
COUGH COUGH
SNIFF!
I KNOW WHAT I CAN MAKE FOR YOU. NOTHING COMPLICATED, REALLY...
IT'S JUST MAGIC...
THERRRE! SHAPING UP NICELY.
THERE...
ER...
GIMME!
GWRB!
WAHOO! I'M IN GREAT SHAPE!
GREAT JOB, NIECE! YOU MAKE THE FAMILY PROUD!... WHAT WAS IT?
WELL... IT WAS SUPPOSED TO BE A POULTICE FOR YOUR FEET...

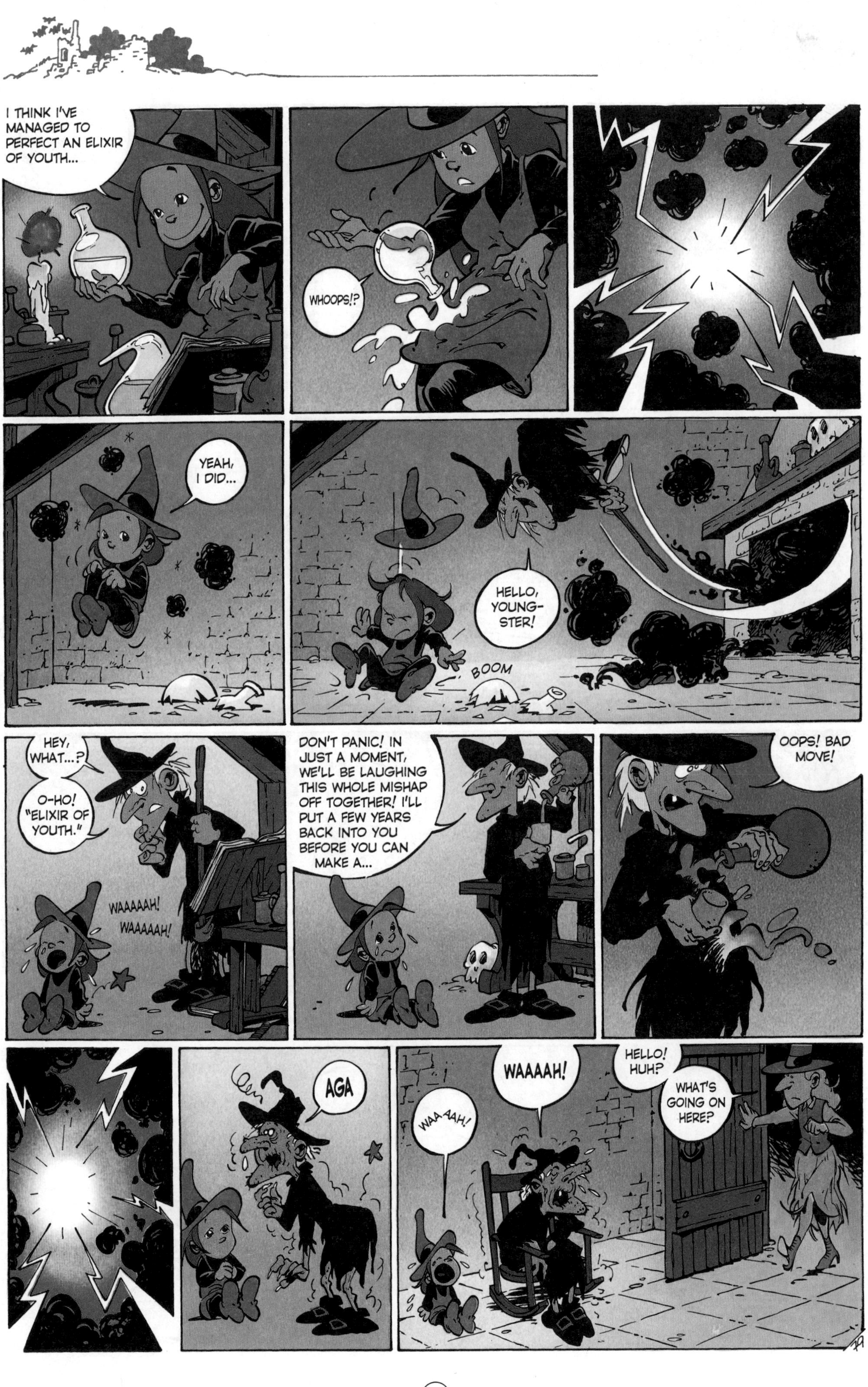
I THINK I'VE MANAGED TO PERFECT AN ELIXIR OF YOUTH...
WHOOPS!?
YEAH, I DID...
HELLO, YOUNGSTER!
BOOM
HEY, WHAT...?
O-HO! "ELIXIR OF YOUTH."
WAAAAAH!
WAAAAAH!
DON'T PANIC! IN JUST A MOMENT, WE'LL BE LAUGHING THIS WHOLE MISHAP OFF TOGETHER! I'LL PUT A FEW YEARS BACK INTO YOU BEFORE YOU CAN MAKE A...
OOPS! BAD MOVE!
AGA
WAAAAH!
WAA AAH!
HELLO! HUH?
WHAT'S GOING ON HERE?

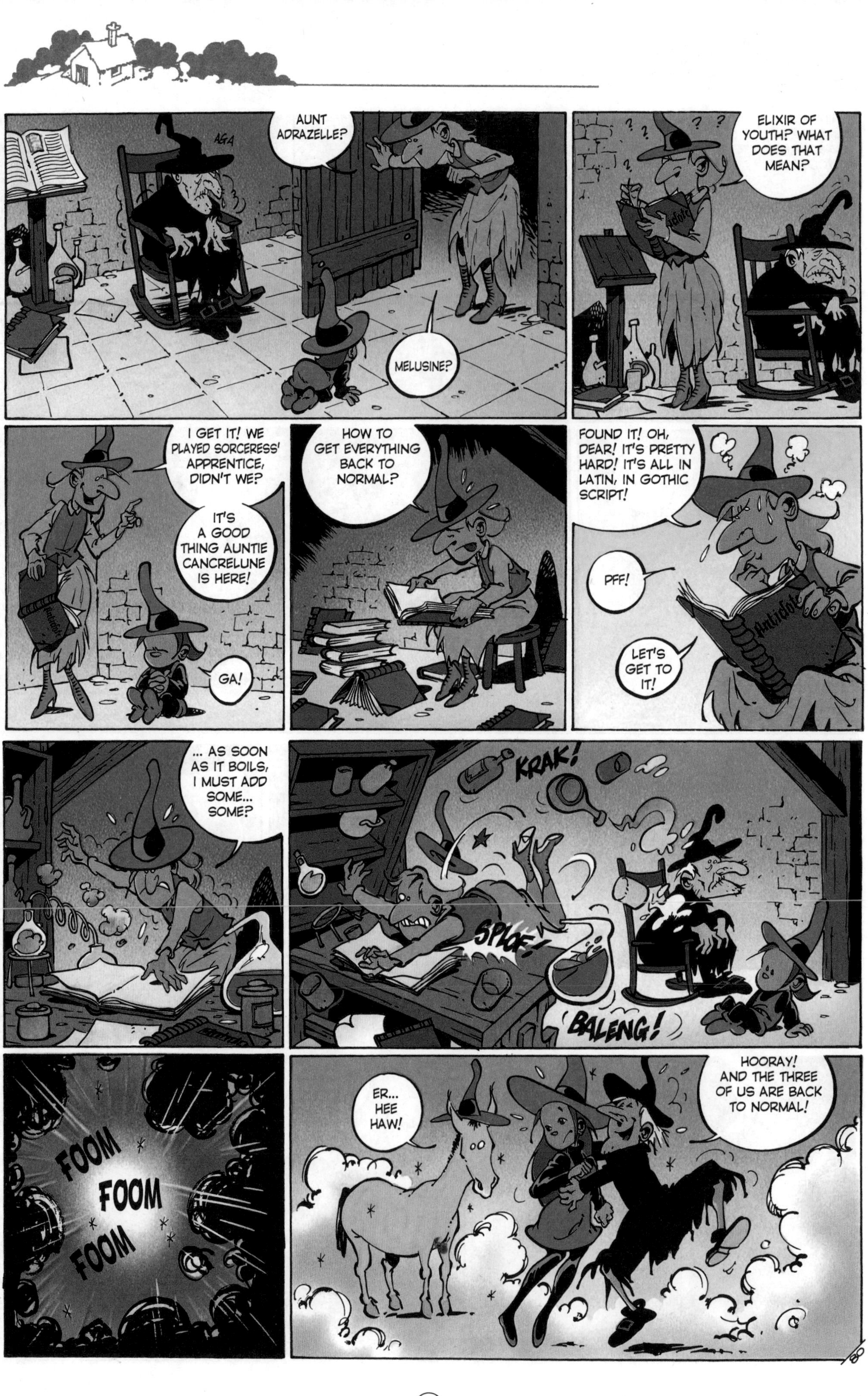
AGA
AUNT ADRAZELLE?
MELUSINE?
ELIXIR OF YOUTH? WHAT DOES THAT MEAN?
I GET IT! WE PLAYED SORCERESS' APPRENTICE, DIDN'T WE?
IT'S A GOOD THING AUNTIE CANCRELUNE IS HERE!
GA!
HOW TO GET EVERYTHING BACK TO NORMAL?
FOUND IT! OH, DEAR! IT'S PRETTY HARD! IT'S ALL IN LATIN, IN GOTHIC SCRIPT!
PFF!
LET'S GET TO IT!
... AS SOON AS IT BOILS, I MUST ADD SOME... SOME?
KRAK!
SPLOF!
BALENG!
FOOM
FOOM
FOOM
ER... HEE HAW!
HOORAY! AND THE THREE OF US ARE BACK TO NORMAL!

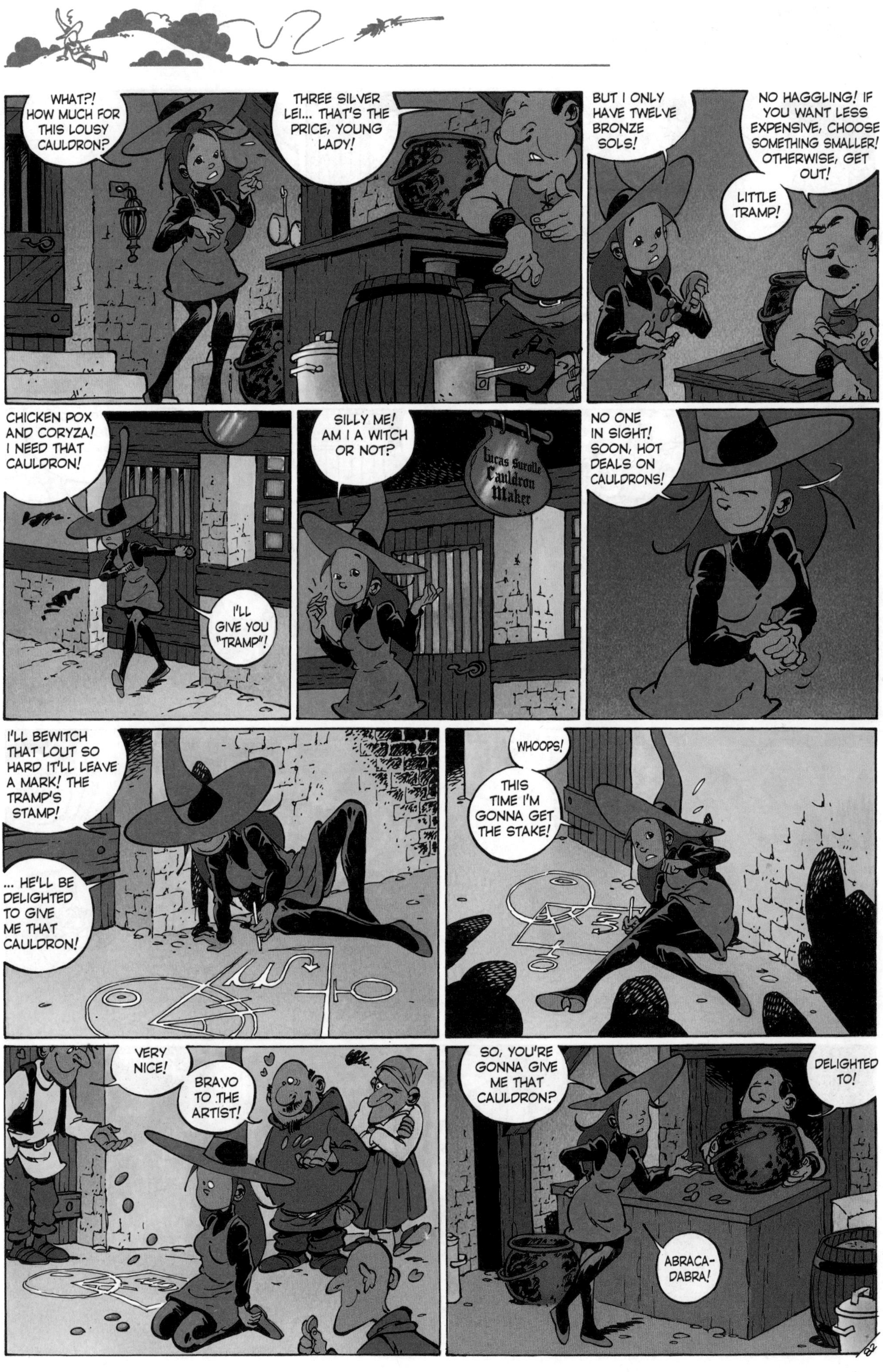
WHAT?! HOW MUCH FOR THIS LOUSY CAULDRON?
THREE SILVER LEI... THAT'S THE PRICE, YOUNG LADY!
BUT I ONLY HAVE TWELVE BRONZE SOLS!
NO HAGGLING! IF YOU WANT LESS EXPENSIVE, CHOOSE SOMETHING SMALLER! OTHERWISE, GET OUT!
LITTLE TRAMP!
CHICKEN POX AND CORYZA! I NEED THAT CAULDRON!
I'LL GIVE YOU "TRAMP"!
SILLY ME! AM I A WITCH OR NOT?
Lucas Surolle Cauldron Maker
NO ONE IN SIGHT! SOON, HOT DEALS ON CAULDRONS!
I'LL BEWITCH THAT LOUT SO HARD IT'LL LEAVE A MARK! THE TRAMP'S STAMP!
... HE'LL BE DELIGHTED TO GIVE ME THAT CAULDRON!
WHOOPS!
THIS TIME I'M GONNA GET THE STAKE!
VERY NICE!
BRAVO TO THE ARTIST!
SO, YOU'RE GONNA GIVE ME THAT CAULDRON?
DELIGHTED TO!
ABRACA-DABRA!

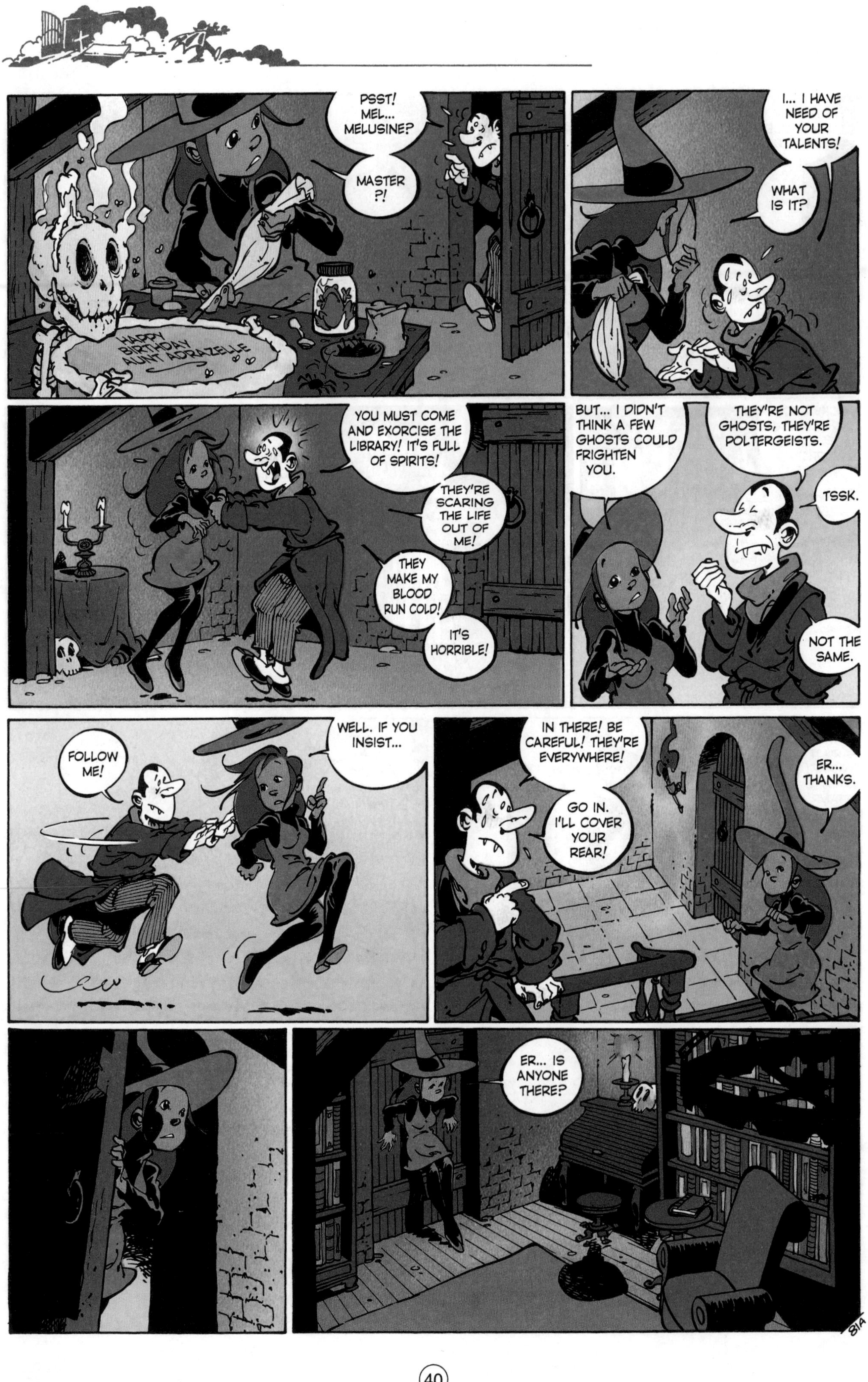
HAPPY BIRTHDAY AUNT ADRAZELLE
PSST! MEL... MELUSINE?
MASTER ?!
I... I HAVE NEED OF YOUR TALENTS!
WHAT IS IT?
YOU MUST COME AND EXORCISE THE LIBRARY! IT'S FULL OF SPIRITS!
THEY'RE SCARING THE LIFE OUT OF ME!
THEY MAKE MY BLOOD RUN COLD!
IT'S HORRIBLE!
BUT... I DIDN'T THINK A FEW GHOSTS COULD FRIGHTEN YOU.
THEY'RE NOT GHOSTS, THEY'RE POLTERGEISTS.
TSSK.
NOT THE SAME.
FOLLOW ME!
WELL. IF YOU INSIST...
IN THERE! BE CAREFUL! THEY'RE EVERYWHERE!
GO IN. I'LL COVER YOUR REAR!
ER... THANKS.
ER... IS ANYONE THERE?
81A

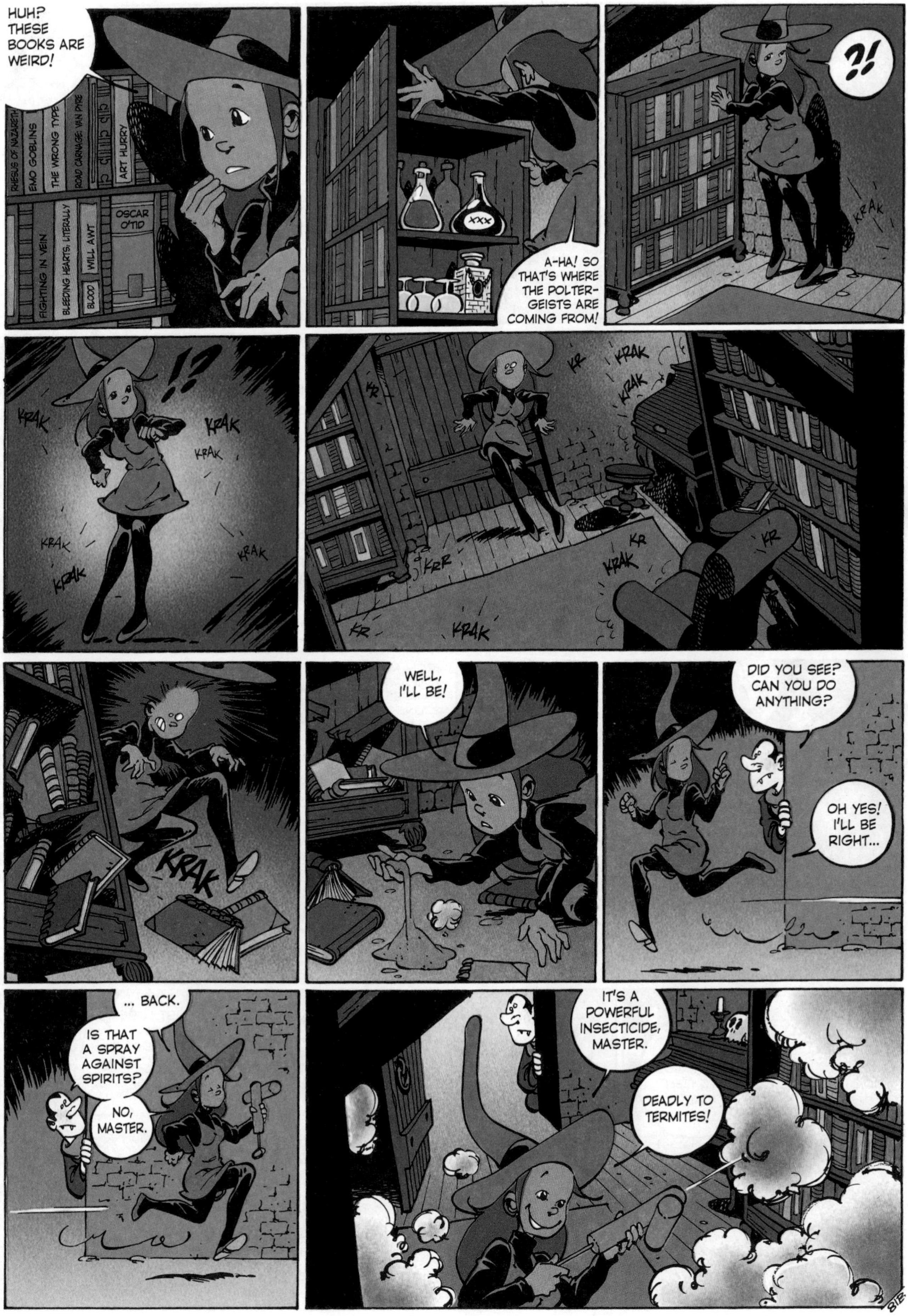
HUH? THESE BOOKS ARE WEIRD!
RHESUS OF NAZARETH
EMO GOBLINS
THE WRONG TYPE
ROAD CARNAGE: VAN PYRE
ART HURRY
FIGHTING IN VEIN
BLEEDING HEARTS, LITERALLY
BLOOD
WILL AWT
OSCAR O'TID
XXX
A-HA! SO THAT'S WHERE THE POLTER-GEISTS ARE COMING FROM!
?!
KRAK
!?
KRAK
KRAK
KRAK
KRAK
KRAK
KRAK
KR
KR
KRAK
KRAK
KRR
KR
KRAK
KR
KR
KRAK
KRAK
WELL, I'LL BE!
DID YOU SEE? CAN YOU DO ANYTHING?
OH YES! I'LL BE RIGHT...
... BACK.
IS THAT A SPRAY AGAINST SPIRITS?
NO, MASTER.
IT'S A POWERFUL INSECTICIDE, MASTER.
DEADLY TO TERMITES!
BIZ

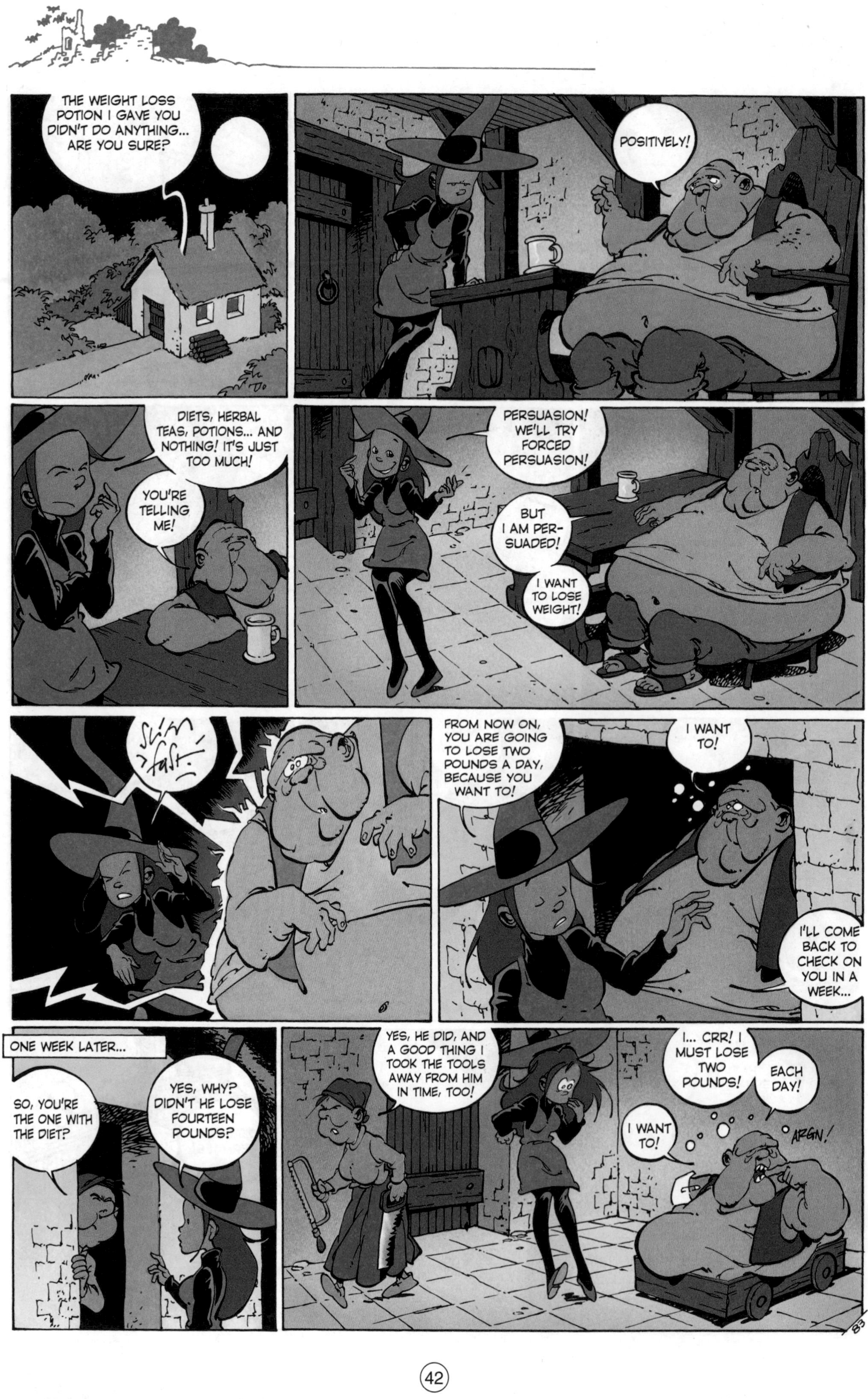
THE WEIGHT LOSS POTION I GAVE YOU DIDN'T DO ANYTHING... ARE YOU SURE?
POSITIVELY!
DIETS, HERBAL TEAS, POTIONS... AND NOTHING! IT'S JUST TOO MUCH!
YOU'RE TELLING ME!
PERSUASION! WE'LL TRY FORCED PERSUASION!
BUT I AM PERSUADED!
I WANT TO LOSE WEIGHT!
FROM NOW ON, YOU ARE GOING TO LOSE TWO POUNDS A DAY, BECAUSE YOU WANT TO!
I WANT TO!
I'LL COME BACK TO CHECK ON YOU IN A WEEK...
ONE WEEK LATER...
SO, YOU'RE THE ONE WITH THE DIET?
YES, WHY? DIDN'T HE LOSE FOURTEEN POUNDS?
YES, HE DID, AND A GOOD THING I TOOK THE TOOLS AWAY FROM HIM IN TIME, TOO!
I... CRR! I MUST LOSE TWO POUNDS!
EACH DAY!
I WANT TO!
ARGN!

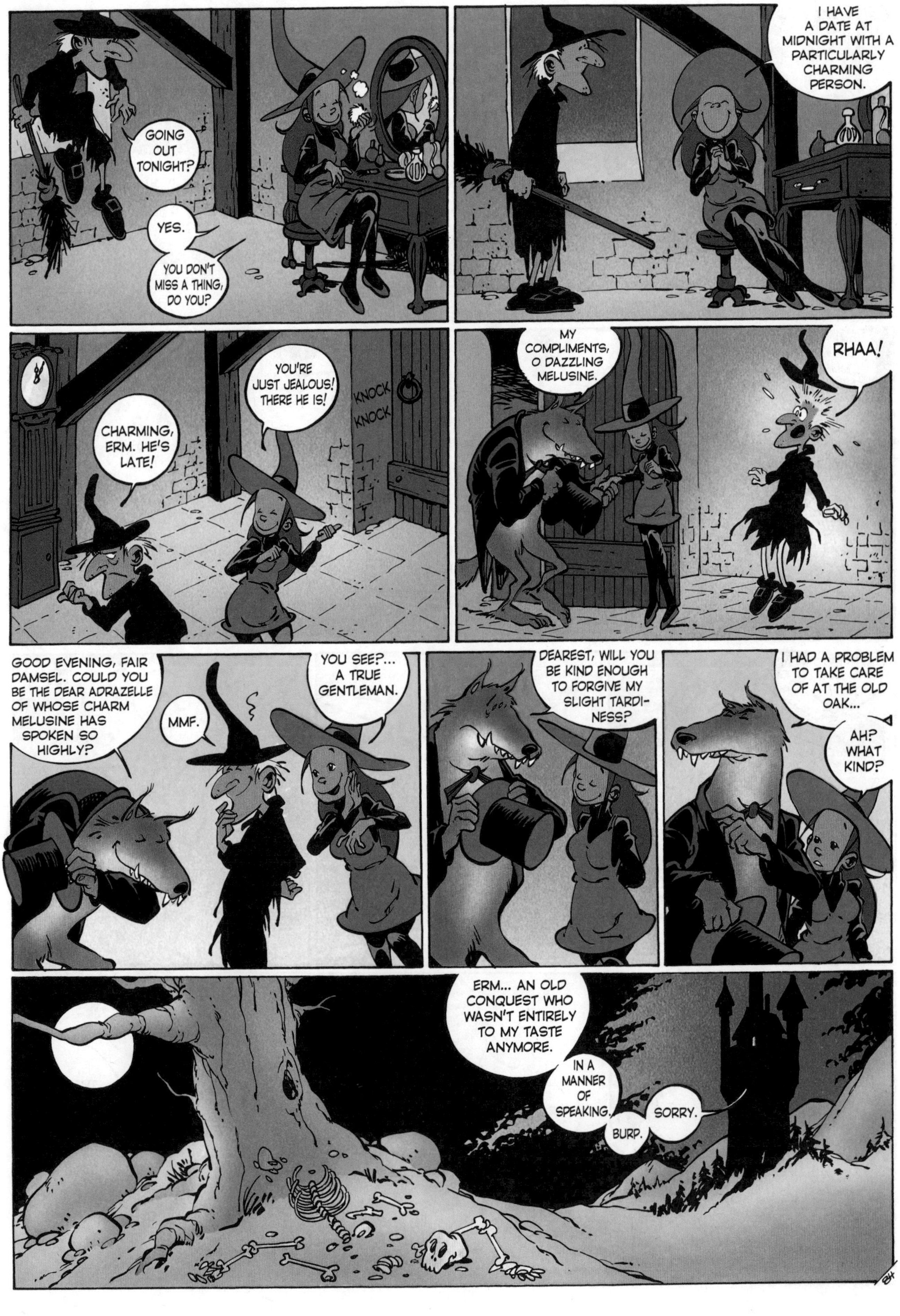
GOING OUT TONIGHT?
YES.
YOU DON'T MISS A THING, DO YOU?
I HAVE A DATE AT MIDNIGHT WITH A PARTICULARLY CHARMING PERSON.
CHARMING, ERM. HE'S LATE!
YOU'RE JUST JEALOUS! THERE HE IS!
KNOCK
KNOCK
MY COMPLIMENTS, O DAZZLING MELUSINE.
RHAA!
GOOD EVENING, FAIR DAMSEL. COULD YOU BE THE DEAR ADRAZELLE OF WHOSE CHARM MELUSINE HAS SPOKEN SO HIGHLY?
MMF.
YOU SEE?... A TRUE GENTLEMAN.
DEAREST, WILL YOU BE KIND ENOUGH TO FORGIVE MY SLIGHT TARDI-NESS?
I HAD A PROBLEM TO TAKE CARE OF AT THE OLD OAK...
AH? WHAT KIND?
ERM... AN OLD CONQUEST WHO WASN'T ENTIRELY TO MY TASTE ANYMORE.
IN A MANNER OF SPEAKING.
BURP.
SORRY.

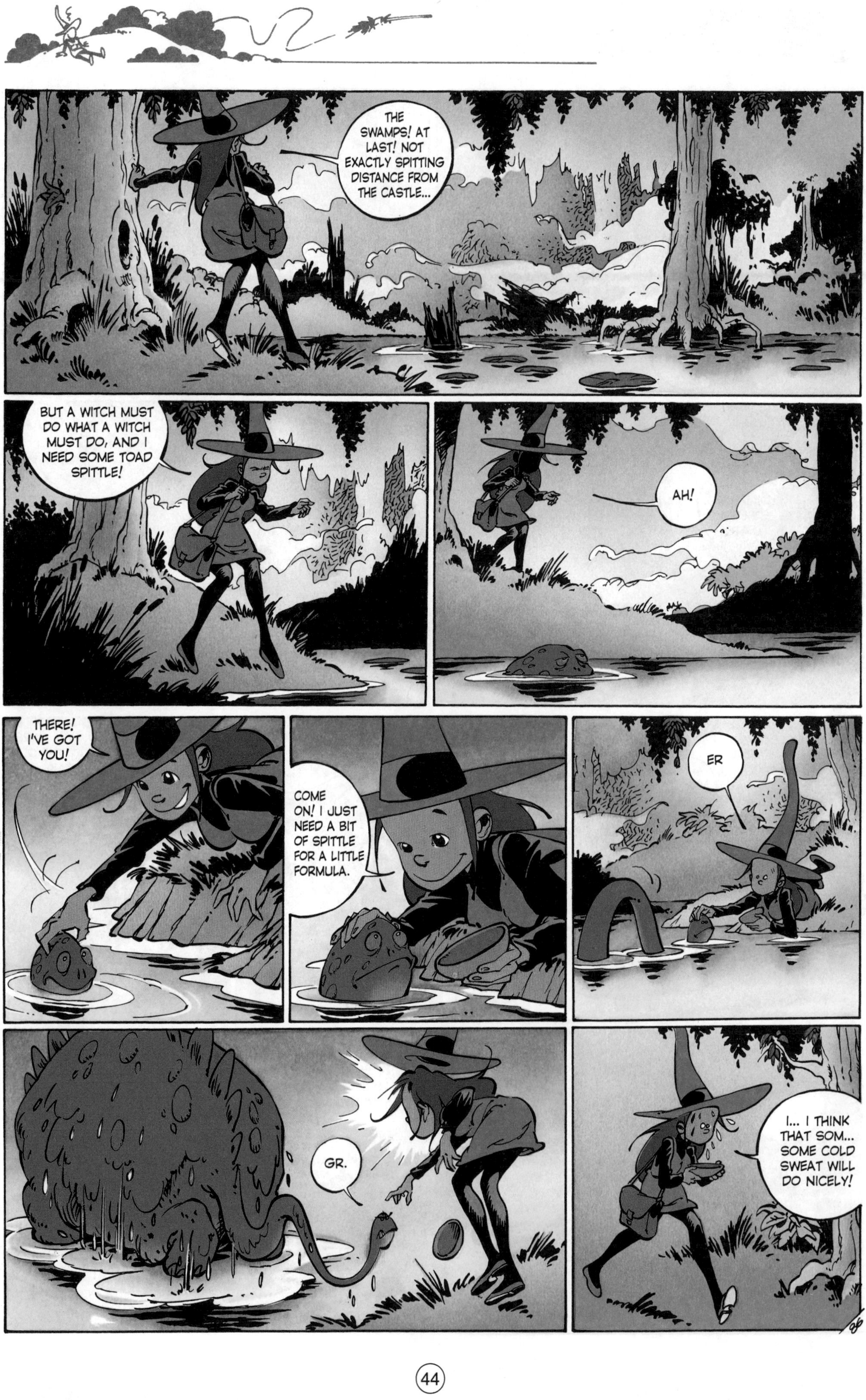
THE SWAMPS! AT LAST! NOT EXACTLY SPITTING DISTANCE FROM THE CASTLE...
BUT A WITCH MUST DO WHAT A WITCH MUST DO, AND I NEED SOME TOAD SPITTLE!
AH!
THERE! I'VE GOT YOU!
COME ON! I JUST NEED A BIT OF SPITTLE FOR A LITTLE FORMULA.
ER
GR.
I... I THINK THAT SOM... SOME COLD SWEAT WILL DO NICELY!

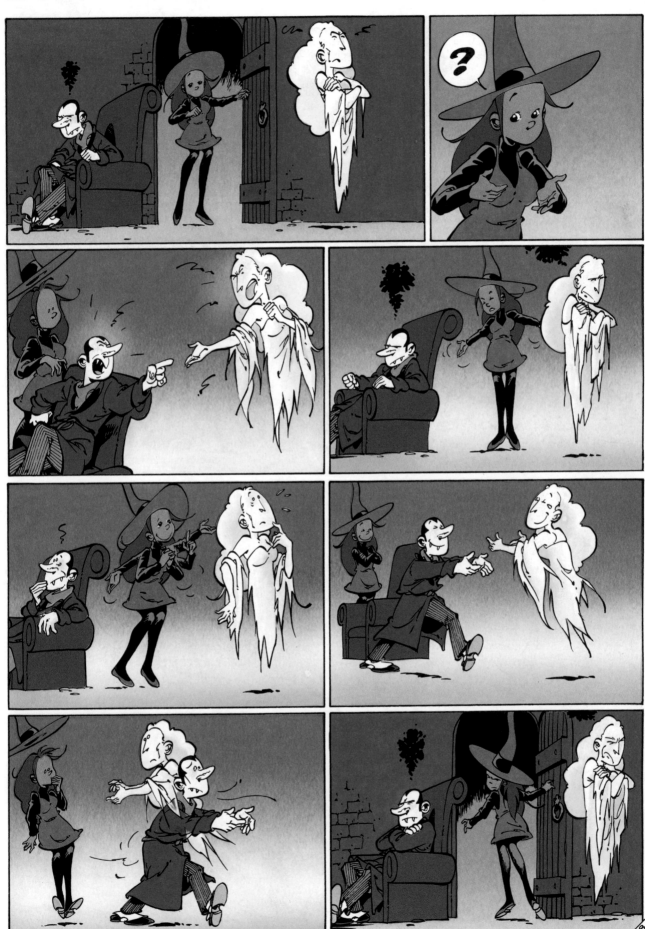

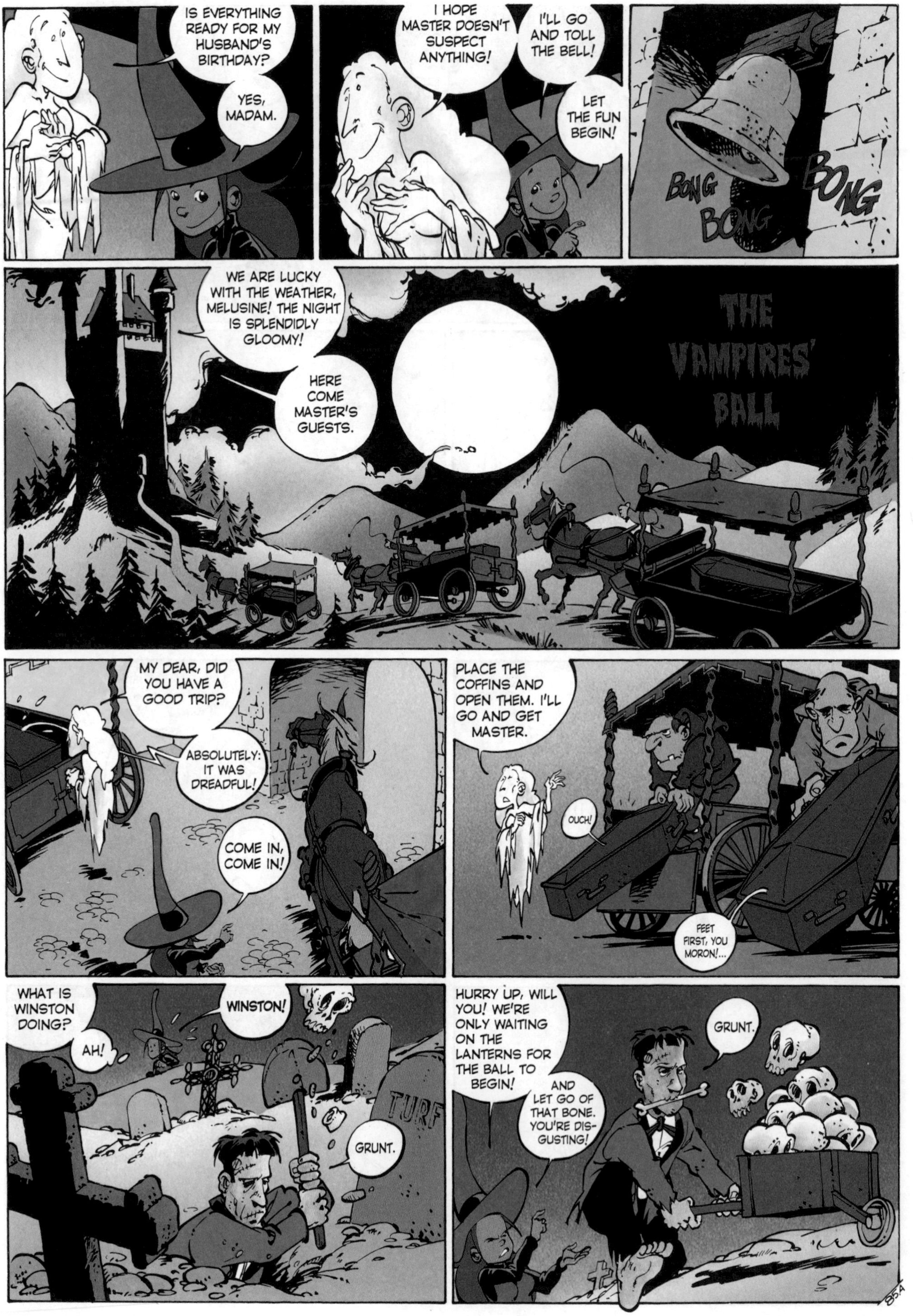
IS EVERYTHING READY FOR MY HUSBAND'S BIRTHDAY?
YES, MADAM.
I HOPE MASTER DOESN'T SUSPECT ANYTHING!
I'LL GO AND TOLL THE BELL!
LET THE FUN BEGIN!
BONG
BONG
BONG
WE ARE LUCKY WITH THE WEATHER, MELUSINE! THE NIGHT IS SPLENDIDLY GLOOMY!
HERE COME MASTER'S GUESTS.
THE VAMPIRES' BALL
MY DEAR, DID YOU HAVE A GOOD TRIP?
ABSOLUTELY: IT WAS DREADFUL!
COME IN, COME IN!
PLACE THE COFFINS AND OPEN THEM. I'LL GO AND GET MASTER.
OUCH!
FEET FIRST, YOU MORON!...
WHAT IS WINSTON DOING?
WINSTON!
AH!
TURF
GRUNT.
HURRY UP, WILL YOU! WE'RE ONLY WAITING ON THE LANTERNS FOR THE BALL TO BEGIN!
AND LET GO OF THAT BONE. YOU'RE DISGUSTING!
GRUNT.

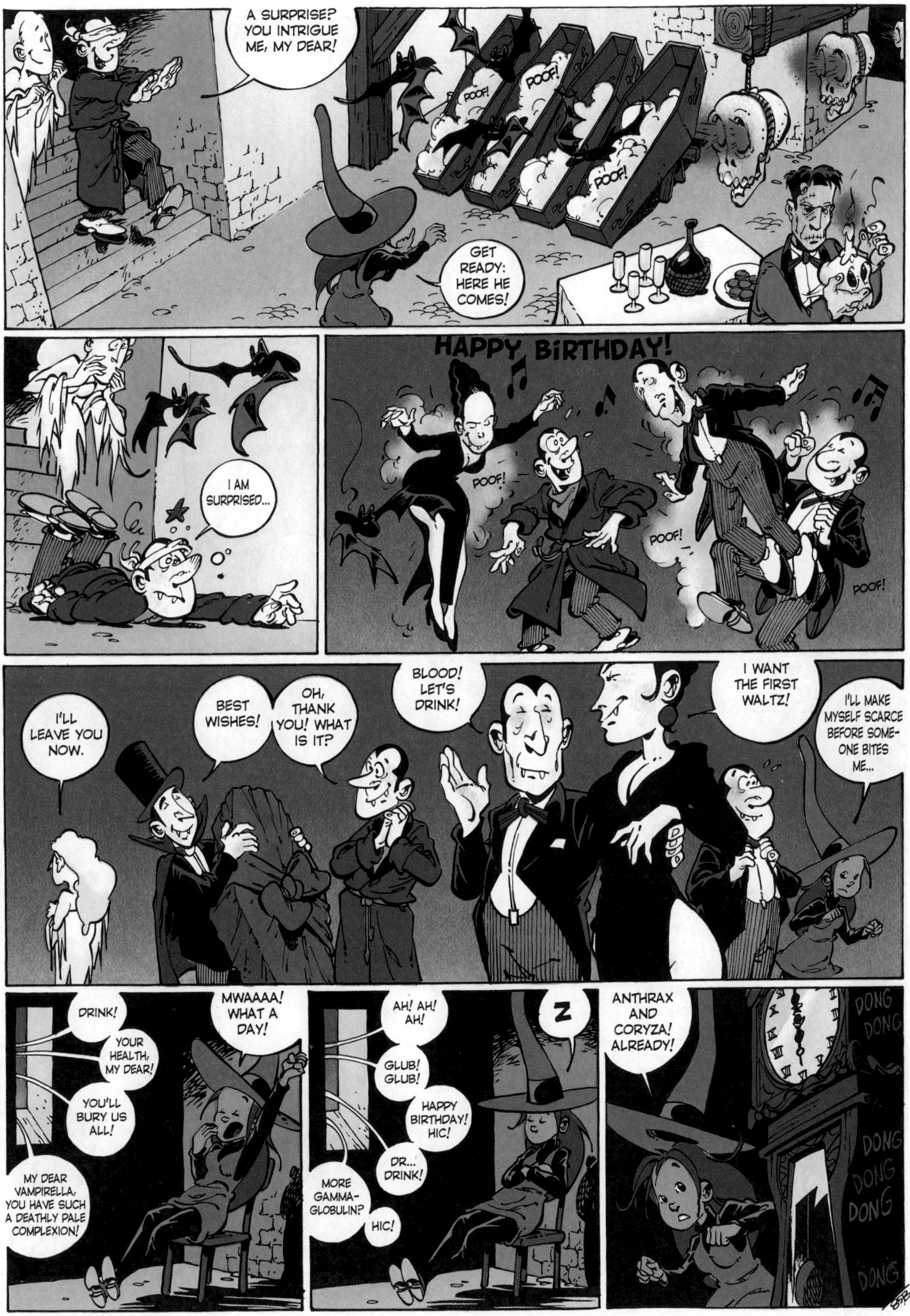

A SURPRISE? YOU INTRIGUE ME, MY DEAR!
POOF!
POOF!
POOF!
GET READY: HERE HE COMES!
I AM SURPRISED...
HAPPY BIRTHDAY!
POOF!
POOF!
POOF!
I'LL LEAVE YOU NOW.
BEST WISHES!
OH, THANK YOU! WHAT IS IT?
BLOOD! LET'S DRINK!
I WANT THE FIRST WALTZ!
I'LL MAKE MYSELF SCARCE BEFORE SOME-ONE BITES ME...
DRINK!
MWAAAA! WHAT A DAY!
YOUR HEALTH, MY DEAR!
YOU'LL BURY US ALL!
MY DEAR VAMPIRELLA, YOU HAVE SUCH A DEATHLY PALE COMPLEXION!
AH! AH! AH!
Z
GLUB! GLUB!
HAPPY BIRTHDAY! HIC!
DR... DRINK!
MORE GAMMA-GLOBULIN?
HIC!
ANTHRAX AND CORYZA! ALREADY!
DONG
DONG
DONG
DONG
DONG
DONG

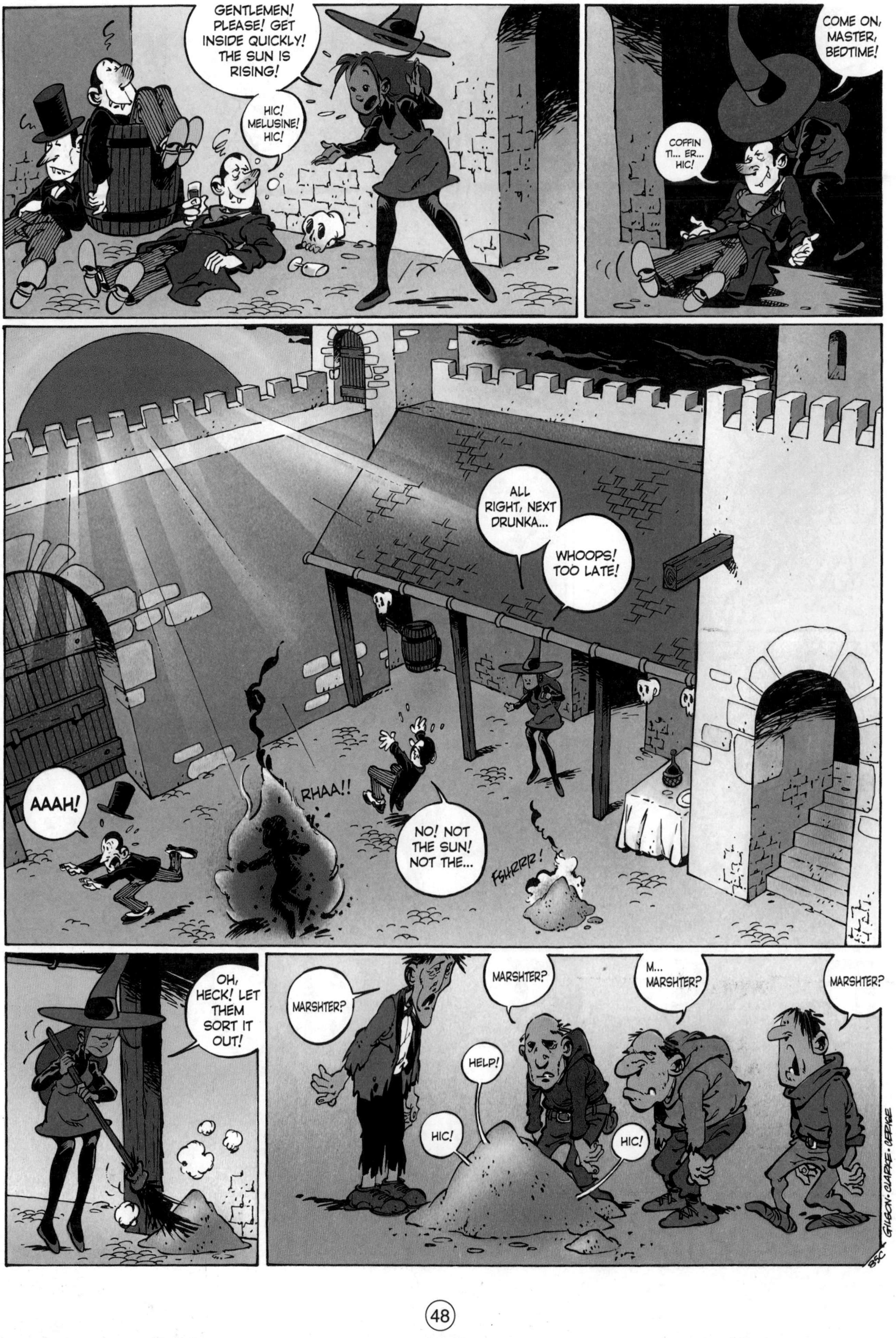
GENTLEMEN! PLEASE! GET INSIDE QUICKLY! THE SUN IS RISING!
HIC! MELUSINE! HIC!
COME ON, MASTER, BEDTIME!
COFFIN TI... ER... HIC!
ALL RIGHT, NEXT DRUNKA...
WHOOPS! TOO LATE!
AAAH!
RHAA!!
NO! NOT THE SUN! NOT THE...
FSHRRR!
OH, HECK! LET THEM SORT IT OUT!
MARSHTER?
MARSHTER?
M... MARSHTER?
MARSHTER?
HELP!
HIC!
HIC!